THA TWINZ
FAMILY SECRETS
BOOK 2

BALTIMORE'S BEST SELLING AUTHOR

KAYO

THA TWINZ II
FAMILY SECRETS
BOOK 2 OF 2

By Kayo

Copyright © 2022 KAYO
All rights reserved.

This is a book of fiction. Any references or similarities to actual events, real people, or real locations, are intended to give the novel a sense of reality. Any similarity to other names, characters, places, and incidents are entirely coincidental.

No part of this book may be reproduced in any form, or by any means, without prior consent of the author/publisher as a collective, except brief quotes used in reviews.

ISBN-13: 9798815980365

Contact Information:
T. Top Publishing
Frienemies400887@gmail.com
IG: @theauthorkayo
FB: Frienemies Author Kayo

Cover Design:
Dynasty's Visionary Designs (Cover Me)
Facebook: www.facebook.com/dynastys.coverme
Email: covermeservice@yahoo.com

Prologue 1

An Abandon Warehouse In South East DC...
Sauce didn't know what to think while he sat, strapped, in the chair inside of a dark, dank, cold building. He didn't know where he was or how long he had been unconscious. He did know someone hit him in his head with a gun when he was on his way to his car.

"What the fuck," he said. "Bitch-ass gang niggas."

Two big guys walked in his line of sight. They didn't have masks on, which was a bad sign to him. They stood in front of him with their arms folded across their chest.

"That shit don't scare me my niggas."

"It ain't us you gotta be scared of," the taller one said.

Sauce was positive he had never seen either one of them before.

"What the fuck ya'll want?" Sauce asked.

"It ain't what we want," the shorter one said. "It's what "she" want."

The taller one put a black, cloth bag over his head. Two minutes later he heard some heels clicking on the floor.

"He say anything?"

"Nothing important."

"Take the bag off his head and just cover his eyes. I need access to his face."

He still didn't see her when they removed the bag, but she was close. He could smell her. His eyes was covered with some kind of cloth that he couldn't see through.

"Okay," she said, walking in front of him, "This is how this is gonna work. I ask the questions. You answer them. If I ask what color you got on, you say white. Not white and why you got on white. You understand me so far?"

"Yeah."

"What's ya name?"

"What?"

The smack was swift, hard, and unexpected.

"I thought you said you understood me?" she asked. "Let's try this again. I ask the questions, you answer me. If I ask you what color do you have on, you answer… what?"

"White."

"I can't hear you."

"White," he said, through clenched teeth.

"We gonna get along real good." She paced the floor, then asked, "What's your name?"

"Sauce."

"Good. You're a natural," she said. "Sauce, did you kill Malik to keep my money?"

"What?"

She punched him in his jaw, ringing his ears.

"Fuck! Just tell me what the fuck you want?"

She threw two more punches. Those got him woozy a bit.

"You fucking up Sauce. I told you how this work," she said and smacked him real hard. "Now, did you kill Malik to keep my money?"

"No."

"Did you kill Malik?"

"No."

"Who killed him then, if it wasn't you?"

"A gang member name Mularu."

"And where does this Mularu be?"

"Twenty-first and Barclay Street."

"Where is my money?"

"I don't know what money you talking about."

She was contemplating was that an answer or not.

"You did business with Malik?"

"Yes."

"So then you were doing business with me, because he worked for me. Understand that. What was Mularu's beef with Malik?"

"They didn't have beef. I don't even think they knew each other."

"So why did he kill him?"

"I'm beefin' with his gang."

"So he got killed because of you?"

"Yes," Sauce said. "Can I say something?"

"Go ahead."

"Mularu is dead. I killed him along with a few more of his gang member friends. I fucked with Malik. He was always good to me."

After he spoke, they left. It felt like an eternity before someone came and fed him a cheese burger and water. Then it was silence again.

"Okay, your story checks out," she said days later when they came back. "You wanna go home? Where's my money? My two hundred thousand dollars?"

He was broken at that point. His once white Versace outfit was soiled with urine and feces. He was beyond mad and wanted to break the woman's neck that put her hands on him. He promised his self he'd find her. But for now, he figured he'd submit.

"I got the money."

"Where, I want it?"

"I'll make the call."

The guy handed her the phone. "Gimmie the number."

She blocked her number and called the number Sauce gave her. It went to voice mail immediately.

"Your boys ain't fucking with you."

"Call back," he said.

She did.

"Yo," he answered.

"Big fella, it's Sauce."

Sauce sat up in bed in a cold sweat. He wiped his forehead and eased out the bed. He didn't want to wake Ko Ko up.

His thoughts was heavy. Last night's events replayed in his head over and over. He could still feel Ivyana's neck in his grasp. He wanted to kill her last night. What he didn't understand was the twins. They were trying to fight him, even after he told them she kidnapped him. Her voice was something he'd never forget. He heard her voice every night in his head, he also felt the smacks and punches.

"Fuck that bitch. I'mma still kill her ass," he said, looking in the mirror.

He didn't want to beef with his childhood friends over Ivyana. Bros before hoes was his motto. He had to convince the twins that she had to go. She needed to die… by his hands.

Chapter 1

AT's home...

When Hondo purchased the home for his aunt; Tamera AT Huntley, he had their whole family in mind. There was a room for him and Honcho, and his mother; Tammy TT Huntley. AT loved having everyone under one roof. She wished they all moved in, but that was a farfetched wish, she knew. Especially her identical twin sister. She knew once her sister got on her feet, she was gonna get her own home. TT was used to her own.

Honcho rolled over in his bed. He sniffed. His stomach growled.
Hondo did the same thing across the hall. The sweet aroma of the breakfast food was assaulting his nose.

Both of them came downstairs in basketball shorts, tank tops, and slippers.
"Good morning my handsome men."
Both boys came over and kissed their mother.
"Morning Momma."
"Hey Momma."
"You don't know how many times in eighteen years that I've thought of this day."
AT came downstairs with rollers still in her hair, but flawless nonetheless.
"Good morning ya'll," she said as she went around kissing everybody. She took a seat at the dining room table with the boys. "What was that shit about last night?"
"I think Sauce had too much Hennessy, AT," Hondo said.

Honcho looked at his brother.

"Sauce was sure she was the one."

"She couldn't have been Momma," he defended. "When Sauce was getting kidnapped, Ivyana was with me in VIP. Think about it bro. She would've had to leave me and get pass ya'll to get to him."

Honcho had a look of relief on his face as he thought about it. "You right bro. Sauce geekin'. She would've had to get pass me and Eeyore. She couldn't have."

"His strong ass tried to kill that girl. Have you talked to her Hondo?"

"Yeah, I talked to her. She's good. She actually wants to see Sauce one on one. "They all exploded in laughter, but Hondo wasn't. "I had the same reaction ya'll, but she's dead ass serious. She doesn't want me or none of us to jump in it."

"You serious bro?"

"Dead-ass."

"My kind of girl," TT said, "but we gotta keep her away from Sauce."

TT brung plates for everyone, and sat down to eat herself.

"So what'chall gonna do about this last guy that was in on the shooting?" TT asked.

The twins looked at each other.

"Don't both of ya'll speak at one time."

Hondo gave his brother a slight head nod.

He sat his fork down, wiped his mouth, and cleared his throat. "Momma, we gotta tell you something."

"You and AT," Hondo added.

Neither one of them knew how to say what needed to be said. They both said it to themselves a lot since finding out, but it still didn't sound right. Almost as if it couldn't be true, but it was. The only people who knew that seven-year-old Hondo was the murderer in the 1999 home invasion, that landed TT in prison, was Hondo, Honcho, TT and the two remaining invaders. The only way Twon could have known was from one of the intruders, because

Hondo, Honcho, and TT never uttered a word about it. AT didn't even know.

"Is one of ya'll gonna talk?" AT asked.

"What was the name of the guy you was locked up for killin', Momma?"

"Antwon Moot, Honcho. You know that. What do he got to do with this?"

Honcho handed his mother the ID he took from Twon's pocket. TT studied it.

"This his son. Where is he?" she asked, handing the ID to her sister.

"He's dead. Gone. We killed him."

"He was one of the shooters out the 'jects."

"What?!" they both screamed simultaneously.

"So, he was on some get back shit?" AT asked.

"Wait. Wait. Wait. Why did he go after you two for? I was the one that killed his father."

"Because Momma, we know you wasn't the one who really killed him."

"What?!" AT yelled. "What the hell is you talking about? You didn't kill him Tammy?" TT shook her head. "You did eighteen years in prison on thirty-six years. Who the hell you went to prison for then?"

"My son, and I'd do it again in a heartbeat."

"I did it AT. I killed him. Momma ate my charge. She went to jail to protect me."

"How come I never knew this?"

"I told them not to say anything to anyone Tamera. They listened to me."

AT looked hurt.

"We sorry AT. We shouldn't have kept it from you."

"Wait. How did this kid know we were involved in his father's murder?"

"Because, his uncle was also in our house with his father. His uncle was the one who gave him the full story of how everything went down."

"The uncle? His uncle was one of the other men."

"And London was the third man."

"And the one who shot our father twice in his head."

"Hold the fuck up!"

"Momma, Twon told us the whole story before we killed him."

"London's bitch-ass set us up and killed my baby," TT said and cried.

AT got up from the table and cried with her sister. The twins had tears falling down their faces as well.

"They're all gonna die. I put that on Clyde's grave," TT vowed.

Chapter 2

Parkwood Cemetery...
They were arm in arm walking to Clyde William Pierce's grave. This was Tammy's first time at her man's grave. She wasn't allowed to attend the funeral, so she had to find another way to grieve.

Clyde's face with his radiant, infectious smile was ingrained on the headstone.

"This is nice Tamera. Very nice."

"These flowers are nice AT."

"I didn't put them there. The last time I was here with flowers was Clyde's birthday. December twenty-fourth."

The ground's keeper rolled around on his buggy cart.

"Hello. I's George. Sorry to interrupt, but ifin yous gonna put those there flowers down on thatin grave right there. I's needs to shows you all hows to dos that there," he said, in a deep southern tongue.

"And how is there a right or wrong way to lay flowers, George?" TT asked.

"The misses will get mad if theys laid the wrong way."

"The misses?"

"Misses Pierce."

They all looked at each other.

"Is this misses a police officer George?" AT asked.

"Yes ma'am. A police she is."

"Thank you George."

"George, it ain't but one Mrs. Pierce, and that's me. That police woman ain't shit. These are Mr. Pierce's only two sons, and they came from me. No one, and I mean no one, dictates this grave right there unless it's one of us," TT said. She went in her bag, pulled out two hundred dollars and gave it to him. She then wrote her number down to the iPhone that Ivyana bought her. "George, if she comes back, you call me ASAP okay?"

"I's sure will Misses Pierce," he said, and rolled away.

"I'm gonna beat that bitch up," TT said. "I'ma teach that bitch about playing with my family."

They stayed at the gravesite for two hours as AT and TT told funny stories about Clyde. The twins enjoyed themselves. They loved to hear about their father.

***

Odonnell Heights Projects…

Walking around the projects didn't even feel the same without Eeyore around. Sauce allowed one tear to escape from his eye. He walked over to the industrial grill that Eeyore bought for Crystal.

"Damn Crystal."

"I miss her too Sauce."

He turned around and saw Eeyore.

"What the fuck! Big fella?"

"You need to make shit right with the twins. They are family."

"But she—"

"No buts. So what she smacked you. You choked her. Ya'll even. Let it go."

"I can't do that."

"You can't do what Sauce?" Shyasia asked.

Sauce looked around for Eeyore.

"You okay Sauce?"

"I'm good," he said, shaking it off. "What's up Shyasia?"

"I was just saying that I miss Eeyore too."

"Yeah, bro was one of ah kind."

"Sauce," she said.

"Yeah."

"I'm pregnant."

Sauce looked at the married woman. "Congratulations."

"It's not my husbands. It's Eeyore's."

"Oh shit, how you know?"

"Two reasons how. I stopped Eeyore from using a condom that last few times we had sex. And the main reason, my husband can't have kids."

"Do your husband know?"

"He's the one that told me. He noticed the changes in my body and said it. I took a test and sure enough, I was."

"What did he say?"

"I told him the baby is a blessing for us. He said he wasn't raising no dead nigga's baby and put me out," she cried.

Sauce pulled her into his chest. "Fuck that nigga, we gon' make sure you good. You can get Eeyore's spot. Let me get all those guns out of there first. You gonna be good Shyasia."

"Thank you Sauce," she cried, hugging him.

Chapter 3

(a week later) Halloween
Mount Pleasant Church...

There was at least forty cars lined up on Radecke Avenue. People came to show their respects to the fallen soldier.

Mourners filed in the church to view the body. The funeral looked like an all gray affair. Everyone definitely respected the deceased gang member's affiliation.

The police was also in attendance; plain clothes and in uniform. They were taking pictures and notes.

The music came on, alerting everyone that the funeral was set to begin.

The pastor gave a sermon on children leaving earth before their parents, the pressures of the streets and gang activity. Sixty-five percent of the mourners could care less, their minds were on retaliation. Whenever a likable, bankable, well known, or high ranking member of the gang was killed, the turn out was big and someone almost always dies afterwards as pay back. It's how things worked in the gang culture.

After the service Mrs. Moots got one last look at her boy and instructed them to close the casket.

Her brother-in-law helped her back to her seat. He locked eyes with a gorgeous female in the fifth row. He knew it wasn't the time or place, but he had to find out who she was.

"The burial will be at the Greemount Cemetery," the pastor told the mourners.

Everyone stood up to leave, as the choir sung Eyes On The Sparrow.

"I'll be right back Kendra," he said.

"Hurry up back Landry. I gotta get to the limo."

He chased the woman down. "Excuse me miss."

She turned around.

"You knew my nephew?"

"Yes. Twon was a friend of mine. I held him down while he was locked up."

"What's your name?"

"Chiquetta. Yours?"

"Landry. You met Twon's mother?"

"No."

"You can meet her tonight at the repast we having at the house."

"Okay. What about his baby mother? He told me she's a little crazy.;'

"You'll be my guest Chiquetta. Here's my number. Don't you worry about nothing. This is for my nephew."

"Okay Landry. See you tonight," she said and walked off. Landry's eyes was glued to her ass.

He shook his head and walked back this his sister-in-law.

The gang members left out first. The gray bandana wearing men, women, boys, and girls poured from the church.

"Fuck the gang!" someone yelled. "And fuck Twon!"

Boom! Boom! Boom! Boom! Boom!

Bocka! Bocka! Bocka! Bocka!

"Fuck the gang!" **Fock! Fock! Fock!**

"Drop the weapons now!" a plain clothed officer yelled.

Fock! Fock! Fock!

Undercover and uniformed officers responded to the gun fire.

Bock! Bock! Bock!

Pure anarchy rained down on the streets. Bodies were everywhere; polices and gang members alike.

***

The media dubbed it Bloody Halloween. Seven gang members was killed. Sixteen was shot. Four police officers was killed. Seven was shot.

The federal government came down on every gang in Baltimore city. Indictments were being unsealed all over the city. Unlike Baltimore City Police, the feds didn't pussy foot around. If your name came up on their gang list or your name was mentioned more than one time in debriefing, they were coming for you. The gang and The Squad; both gangs that were responsible for Bloody Halloween, were hit the hardest.

The gang members that didn't get caught up in the fed's sweep were hiding out, too afraid to make any noise.

Chapter 4

Mo's Seafood Restaurant...

Hondo wasn't hungry, so he just ordered a drink. Sauce came in hoping to resolve their issues. He spotted Hondo at the table.

Neither man exchanged peasantries.

"Where you been?'

"Chillin' Hondo. Gettin' my shit together."

"You ain't even call to tell us about Shyasia. She almost got her ass shot in Eeyore's spot."

"We wasn't talking."

Hondo looked at Sauce crazy. "What we some bitches Sauce? We ain't talking? Nigga we came up in the sandbox together."

"That's what I'm saying. Hondo, your bitch had me kidnapped. She put her hands on me. If that was any other bitch she would've been in the dirt."

(Sighs) "She said it wasn't her bro. You never saw her face,. You said that."

"Bro, I sat binded to a fuckin' chair, for two weeks, shittin' and pissin' in my all white Versace linen. Blindfolded. I know her voice. I will never forget it. It was her. I'm sure it was her."

"From her voice bro? Come on Sauce."

Sauce shook his head. "I see ya'll took care of that Twon situation," he said changing the subject. He didn't want to beef with Hondo about it. Honcho would understand better.

"Yeah, but that Halloween shit was wicked. Glad we ain't get caught up in that shit."

"They killed polices too."

"I heard," Hondo said.

It got awkwardly quiet after their exchange.

"So how we gonna carry it Hondo?" he said, after five minutes.

"I 'on't know Sauce. I'll just keep her away from you."

"Keep her away?" laughed Sauce. "Yo, this bitch put her… you know what, fuck it." Sauce got up and left.

"Shit," Hondo said, knowing he was dead wrong… but love was a motherfucker.

***

Parole & Probation…

"Huntley! Huntley!"

"Hold my bag," Tammy said and passed her bag off.

She walked upstairs with her parole officer and into her office.

"Hello Ms. Huntley."

"Hey," she said, nonchalantly.

"Any trouble?'

"No."

"Contact with the police? Any new arrest?"

"No and no."

Miss Hodges looked at Tammy's pricey attire.

"Do you have a job Ms. Huntley?"

"Yes, I work at Sister's Haven Bar & Lounge out Yale Heights."

Her PO was taking notes. "Have you paid your fine?"

"The money order is in my bag. I was going to pay it on my way out."

"No address change?"

"No."

"See you next week."

"Miss Hodges."

"Yes."

"I want to put in for a transform to Moument Street."

"You mind if I ask why?"

"It's closer and it's safer. I don't feel safe coming up here." Tammy said. "I've been away from my sons for eighteen years. I don't wanna be away from them again and forever from getting hit by a stray bullet."

"I can't argue with that. I'll put the transfer request in. Have a good day Ms. Huntley."

"You too," she said and spent on her Cristian Louboutin shoes and left.

"Let's go girl," she said, grabbing her purse from Ivyanna.

"What did she say Momma TT?"

"She act like she gonna put it in. I 'on't know girl. That bitch act like she don't like me or something. She gon'' look me up and down and ask me do I got a job." She laughed. "Yeah bitch I got on seven hundred dollar shoes and a thousand dollar outfit. Shit, I been locked up years bitch, umma flex. Forty-five years old and all."

"I know that's right Momma TT."

"He call that burn out yet?"

"When has he not called? He's been blowing the phone up."

"This is gonna be too easy. Landry ain't gonna have a clue. Silly-ass nigga," Tammy said, shaking her head. "What's up with you and my son?"

"What do you mean Momma TT?"

"My son never introduced no female to me… ever. He loves you. That much is obvious, but what about you?"

"I love Hondo too. I know we haven't' been together long, but I'm in love with him too."

Tammy looked at her. That pretty face masked a lot of pain, she could tell.

"Let me tell you why "I" like you. You are hiding a lot of pain and hurt behind that pretty face and those green eyes. I've been in your shoes. I know what pain feels like, I also know what it look like," she said, causing a tear to trickle down Ivyana's eye. "You don't trust my son enough, yet, to open that closet, but you will. My son is loyal, both of them. And that's why Sauce isn't dead for putting his hand on you. Those boys; my sons, Sauce and big baby Eeyore, grew up together.

"Now, I'll tell you this, my son loves you, so automatically I love you. But Honcho is a different story. He's not so loving and trusting. He's gonna respect you, because of his brother, but he's not gonna rest until he finds out the truth about Sauce's kidnapping.

"I'm not worried Momma TT. I didn't do it or have anything to do with it."

"I believe you sweety."

Chapter 5

Honcho was fussing to no one at all about the domestic work he had to put in at his house. He didn't enjoy that part of living alone, but it had to be done because he hated a dirty house. He made plans to ask his mother to come stay with him until she got back on her feet.

He flipped the Balmain jeans upside down and a bunch of stuff fell out. This was the third pair of jeans he flipped that pockets were full. He picked the stuff up and found a driver's license, money, gum wrapper, and a few pieces of paper with numbers on it.

He flipped the license over and smiled. "Jerell McKinny." Honcho put the license in his pocket and finished his work.

***

Maryland Correctional Institution of Jessup (MCIJ)...

London and Slimbob walked the track and discussed business ventures and recent events. Neither man said it, but both of them feared that sometime soon the feds would come and grab them up and put them on one of the many gang indictments that was coming down.

"So you're gonna keep it up," London said.

"Long as the bitch don't start trippin'."

"She good. I got her in compliance. She's gonna move for me as long as she getting paid well."

"That ain't no problem London."

"Listen homie, she's no fool. Do not try to run game on her or try to change her fee or be late paying. You do this right, ya'll gon be good."

"I got this bro. Good lookin' out." Slimbob said. "So what'chu gon' do when you get out there?"

"I'm forty-seven years young. I'm going out there to put a baby in a bad ass twenty-year-old." They laughed. "Of course I'mma get to that bag."

"Facts."

"I'm not fuckin' with none of our goofy-ass brothers."

"Shit, is there anyone left?"

"You know they ain't get everybody. It don't matter, I'm not fuckin' with them if they ain't tryna get no money."

"I hear you," he said. "You gotta watch out for The Squad."

"Fuck The Squad, they better watch out for me. I'm not worried about them broke ma'fuckas!"

"Right, just be careful."

"Okay. I will."

"Whata'chu think about the feds grabbing the old man?" Slimbob asked.

"He had too many people writing him. That's why when I wrote to him I did it through a female. I'm glad I did too."

"Damn, I hope they don't fuck with me. I only got two years left."

"Fcuk them peoples. I'm outta here soon," he said. "Outta here."

***

Washington, DC…
(17th Street) NW
So run up, run up, run up
Hoe get done up
And you know I'm with the shits

Don't tolerate no disrespect
This Dexter Ave, in this bitch
You might wanna reconsider me
Before you make your choice
Cause if you niggas bet against me
Then you backing the wrong horse...

Ivyana was rapping the lyrics to Kash Doll's song Check when her sister came in. She turned the music down when her sister sat on her bed.

"What's up love?"

"Nothing, worried about you Ivy."

"I'm fine."

"You sure?" she asked. "Have you seen that nigga?"

"No. Hondo not gonna let that nigga around me."

"So what we gon' do about him putting his hands on you sis? 'Cause something gotta be done."

"Let it go Love. Chalk it up to the price of war."

Her sister looked at her with a side eye. "You love this nigga Hondo. My lil' sister is in love!"

"Shut up," she laughed. "I do love him, that's why I wanna let this shit go about this nigga Sauce. Hondo believed me when I told him it wasn't me who kidnapped him and that's all that matters."

Her sister shook her head. "I understand you love him, that's cool, but don't be stupid. A nigga put his fuckin' hands on you Ivy. Let's not forget about the last nigga who tried that shit."

"I know Love. It won't happen again."

"It better not."

Ivyana threw two stacks of money on the bed next to her sister.

"What's this?"

"I sold the Mercedes on the lot."

"No you didn't!"

"I did," Ivyana said.

"I gotta go back to the auction then."

"Business is good."

***

1200 Block of Summit Avenue…

Honcho sat inside his Range Rover Velar. The dark green exterior helped conceal the truck under the night's sky. He was watching house 1206. He checked the license once more to make sure he was right.

He was tired of waiting, so he got out, checked his weapon, and approached the house.

Honcho didn't know what he was doing or what he planned to accomplish, but he wanted to try, so he knocked.

Knock. Knock. Knock.

A nice looking woman came to the door holding a toddler in her arm.

"May I help you?"

"Jerell home?" Honcho asked.

"Who are you?" she asked, looking him skeptically.

"A friend."

"Does this friend have a name?"

"Jo Jo."

"I don't know you Jo Jo. Never even heard of you. So I suggest you leave here and never come back."

"Who is it ba—" he was saying before locking eyes with Honcho.

"Like I said, my name is Jo Jo and I'm a friend of Jerell's."

"Ahh ahh babe. I got this. He cool. Take the baby in the house."

His wife went in the house reluctantly, then he came out and closed the door.

"Yo, what are you doing here?"

"I didn't have your number," Honcho smiled.

"It's not funny. My wife is a police officer."

"I didn't come here on no bullshit. We got our homeboy back."

"So why are you here?"

"Here," he said, handing him his license back. "You won't ever see me again, unless I come back to BWX."

"I quit the same night you pistol whipped me unconscious," Jerell said.

"Okay, you won't ever see me again."

"Good."

"Before I go, I need you to do one thing for me."

"I knew it was more to it."

"Shut up. This is easy," he said pulling out his phone. "Tell me if either one of these girls is the one that paid you the thousand dollars."

He showed Jerell a photo of the two girls that Sauce was with right before he got kidnapped.

"No. I did see them that night, but neither one of them is the one I'm talking about."

"Swipe left."

One look at the photo and he said, "That's her."

"You sure?"

"I'm sure."

"Look again Jerell."

"I'm telling you, it's her. Look at her, who forgets that face? I sure didn't.

Five minutes later Honcho was back in his truck on his way back to the city. The picture of Ivyana was still illuminated on his phone, sitting on the passenger seat.

"Lying bitch," he said, shaking his head.

Chapter 6

The next day Honcho got his mother reacquainted with the projects, since she'd be running the dope out there. Tammy wasn't one to waste time, she wanted her business to boom asap. Honcho showed his mother the crew that would be working for her. She immediately gave him the scrunched up face she and her sister was known for.
"What's wrong Momma?"
"I don't know them. And I don't work with people I don't know."
Honcho didn't know what to do. He didn't want to fire Eeyore's workers.
"Is there any other dope out here?"
"Not as good as ours."
"How much was Eeyore doing a day?"
"Twenty to twenty-five bands ah day."
Tammy calculated the numbers in her head and said, "Call them over here."
Honcho called the three young boys over to them.
"Yo, listen. This woman—"
"Which one of ya'll got money saved up from working with Eeyore?" she asked, with no time to be pussy-footing around.
One boy raised his hand.
"What's ya name sweety?"
"Samo."
"I knew just from looking at you that you were the saver," she said. "Which one of ya'll got at least sixty dollars in your pockets right now?"
Samo raised his hand and the other kid.

"What's your name?"

"German."

"German? Okay. And your name?"

"Batman."

She smiled. "Batman, you have no money saved up and you don't have at least sixty dollars in your pocket. Honcho, pull your money out, you do the same German and Samo."

They listened.

"Now pull out what you have Batman."

He put his head to the ground.

Tammy raised his head up. "Look at me. And listen, 'cause this is the best advice you gonna get for free," she said. "Find you a grind. Without it, you won't be shit. You were out here taking up space young man. I can't use you on my team. You don't have no grind. Get some and come back and see me."

Batman walked away with his head down.

"Samo, German, don't ever let me catch you with less than sixty dollars in your pockets; ever, or you'll be with your homeboy.

"This operation ain't no game. Prison ain't a game. So I won't have games around me. I'm bringing two women in that's gonna help us and we gonna get this money.

"Last chance to leave," she said.

No one moved.

"Let's get this money. I'll see ya'll in two days right here."

"Your pep talk is better than Phil Jackson's, Momma," he said, when they walked away. "I wanna come work for you now."

"Shut up Honcho. Where's your brother?"

"The mall."

"What's on our mind?" she asked.

"How you know something on my mind?"

"Don't make me smack the shit outta you Honcho."

(Sighs) "You ever knew something that would hurt AT and didn't know if you should tell her?"

"Yup. My sister loved London's bitch-ass. I tolerated him because he was your father's best friend and my sister loved him. I was the one who caught him and Sandra together."

"What did you do Momma?"

"What a real sister should've done; I told her. I knew she loved that nigga, but my sister's feelings meant more to me. I told her, she cried, I cried, we cried, then once we were cried out, we beat that nigga's ass… with baseball bats. We broke his arm and one of his legs. We sent his bitch-ass right to the hospital," she said. "Why you ask me that? You caught Ivyana doing something she wasn't supposed to be doing?"

(Sighs)

"Let it out Honcho."

"She kidnapped Sauce, Momma."

"What?"

"She did it."

"She looked me in my eyes and lied to me. She lied to my son," she said. "I liked this bitch too."

Honcho gave her the whole rundown of everything that happened.

"That was smart of you to hold on to that license," she said when he was done.

"Yeah, it came in handy," he said.

"She could've just came out and said she did it. It wasn't too much damage done. I mean, Sauce's pride is hurt, but he could've got over it with my help. By her lying, it puts a whole nother shade on it. I hate liars and I'm not about to have my son dating a liar."

"So tell'em?'

"You better. We don't know this bitch like that."

"Momma, this gonna crush his soul. He really loves that girl."

"Honcho, we are your brother's eyes and ears. It's our duty to—"

"What if I'm wrong?"

"Don't be silly. You said the bouncer from BWX recognized her as the one that paid him the thousand dollars. Unless he's not sure."

"I wish he wasn't sure Momma, but he was. He recognized her immediately."

"Hondo might kill that bitch," he said. "Call his phone."

Chapter 7

Hondo looked at his phone and sighed. He didn't want any interruptions. He hit the end button, knowing if it was important his brother would call back. He didn't, so he continued fixing his room up. Pleasure was the name of today's game and he had just that in store for Ivyana.

After the last candle was in place, Hondo hopped in the shower and bathed with the Axe body wash and sponge.

At ten pm he got a text from Ivyana saying she was ten minutes away. He put on his Gucci Robe and slippers with nothing else on and waited downstairs with an all black scarf in his hand.

She showed up at his door, as requested, in something casual and bright smile.

"Hey baby. You looking mighty fine in that robe. Got anything on under it," she asked, going in for a kiss.

He stopped her.

"Ooop," she said, surprised.

"You trust me?"

She looked in his serious eyes. "I do."

"You prove it tonight," he said, bringing the scarf from behind his back. She looked at the scarf, then at him, and turned around. *Damn I love this girl,* he thought. He tied it around her eyes from behind and took her by the hand. When they got to the steps he picked her up and carried her to his bedroom.

He put her down, lit the candles, and put on some music.

"Damn it smell good in here baby," she said.

I like it when you lose it
I like it when you go there
I like the way you use it
I like that you don't play fair
Recipe for a disaster
When I'm just tryna take my time
Stroke is getting deep and faster
Screaming like I'm outta line

Hondo removed the scarf. She looked around the room. Candles, rose petals, a bowl of ice, a bowl of mixed fruit, Rose' Perrier - Jouet champagne, whip cream and some other fun items. She knew she was about to experience the best sex of her young twenty-four-year-old life.

When we fuck
When we fuck
He ripped her shit off.
When we fuck
Her bra was next to go.
When we fuck

He looked her in her sexy green eyes when Tank sung;

I could be aggressive
I can be a savage
I just need your blessing
Say that I can have it, yeah

"You can have it baby. You have my blessing," she said, breathlessly.

Who came to make sweet love, not me
Who came to kiss and hug, not me

Who came to beat it up, Rocky
And don't use those hands to put
up that gate and stop me

Hondo easily tore her leggins off the bottom half of her body. Her breathing patterns exposed her emotions. He could literally feel her body heating up in his hands.

You end up call me master
Say this universe is mine
"It's your daddy," she said, shaking under his touch.
When we done it's a disaster
End up like this every time
He removed his robe, exposing his excitement.
When we fuck
When we fuck

Hondo grabbed her leg up. She caught on and jumped up wrapping her legs around his waist as he placed himself inside of her aqua wet box.

When we fuck
When we fuck

Both of them let themselves completely go and gave way to the animalistic side of themselves. They were wild, thrashing around the floor, the bed, the chair, in the air, upside down and other ways imaginable. They were savages. Hondo threw her on the bed and crawled between her legs, but not before grabbing a hand full of grapes. He put seven grapes inside of her. Hondo licked her lower lips. They were pulsating under his tongue from the pounding he gave them.
"Bite it," she said

Hondo bit down on her clitoris; 'causing her to scream and cum one great big orgasm. He sucked the cum covered grapes right out of her as she came.

She had a hard time catching her breath after that orgasm, but Hondo wasn't done with her yet. He grabbed the bowl of fruit and the whip cream and placed Ivyana on all fours.

Face down ass up
Back, back, back it up

Hondo laced her lower back with whip cream and stuck a strawberry in her but halfway.

Let me get both of them legs
And put'em both behind your head
This shit getting' deep, deep up in here
Feel your legs getting weak up in here
Get a face full of that gushy, I'm close
baby don't push me, this is how it
always should be when
When we fuck

He entered her from behind, grabbed her hips and plowed inside of her.

"Ahhhh! Hon-do! Ye-ye-yes!"

Her cries only fueled him to go harder. He gave it to her hard causing her to grip the sheets tight. "Sh-sh-sh-it!" She came again.

Hondo sped up, feeling his orgasm ascending. She felt it too, so she threw her phat ass back on him. On contact their flesh was sounding like a smack in the face… repeatedly.

"Agghhhh!" Hondo roared as he came deep inside her womb. "Shit." He pulled out of her, leaned over and licked her back clean of whip cream.

"Ummm," she said. Just when she thought he was done, he opened her big ass open and ate the strawberry out of her butt."

He shared the strawberry with her through a deep passionate kiss and she accepted it lovingly.

They both collapsed on the bed side by side exhausted.

"Is this what I have to look forward to baby?"

"This and much more."

"We may as well get married now then," she said, laughing.

Hondo got up, poured them glasses of the champagne and handed her one.

She looked at her man through squinted eyes and said, "This ain't over, is it?"

(Smiling) "Nope."

She laid up on him while he sat up on the head board. His arm was around her fondling her right breast. She began fondling him. His reaction was immediate.

Ivyana got an idea. She swallowed her drink and grabbed the fruit bowl.

"I love you Hondo Pierce."

"Do you mean that?"

"With everything in me," she said, confidently.

"I love you too Ivyana Richardson."

"Do you mean that," she countered, spooning some pineapples out.

"Every word of it."

She placed the pineapples in her mouth and then on him. The pineapple was cold on him, but her mouth quickly warmed him. She moved up and down on him slowly at first, then gradually moved faster.

"Oooh," he said, "shit."

She grabbed the base of him and sucked on the helmet. Hondo's toe curled as she performed. Ivyana put on an Oscar worthy performance. She took it out her mouth and kissed it, then rubbed it over her lips and face.

Hondo just looked at her, stuck in a trance. After making contact with every inch of her face, she put it back in her mouth to deep throat him. She went ham on him.

"Agghhh! Fu-uck!" he growled. "Ahhh, umm."

He came and she didn't budge, she caught it. Once she was sure he was done, she raised her head and opened her mouth.

"Damn babe," he said, looking at all the cum covered pineapples.

She chewed them up and swallowed them. She opened her mouth to show him that everything was gone and ran to the bathroom.

Ten minutes later he was in a deep sleep. She came out of the bathroom and smiled.

"Put that ass to sleep huh," she laughed, got in the bed and fell asleep on him.

Hondo woke up the next morning with Ivyana's naked body entwined in his. *I could get use to this,* he thought. He stayed still for a long time, not wanting to move.

His phone vibrated. He tried to ease out of her clamps, but she woke up.

"Good morning."

"Great morning," she said and kissed his lips.

He grabbed his phone.

"Yeah, who this?"

"This Civil my nigga."

"Yoooo. What's up man?"

"I got your new number from Sauce. I need you. It's a big game Saturday. Some Atlanta niggas in town that wanna play."

"You know these Atlanta niggas?"

"No, but Reese do. He said he went up there last summer and played them niggas."

"How much is the purse?"

"Seventy bands per man."

"Seventy bands per man," Hondo repeated and thought about it. "Okay, I'm down."

"You good Hondo?"

"I'm good," he said, remembering the bullets that tore through him months ago. "Where we playing at?"

"We playing on the inside."

"I'm there, but we coming hard. You know the streets ain't right."

"Come how you come bro. You gotta protect yourself. Just make sure we win this game."

"Got'chu," he said and ended the call.

Ivyana was looking at him smiling.

"What?"

"Do I finally get to see you do what you love to do?"

"You wanna come see me play?"

"You know I do."

"Well, I guess you gon' see ya man do him."

"You ain't nice," she teased.

"Shittin' me. Niggas know how I give it up."

Hondo was excited and didn't give two thoughts about Sauce being there. His mind was on showing off Saturday for his girl.

Chapter 8

Central Police Department...
Detective Woody marked a file 'case closed' and placed it in a box. His partner, Detective Altman came up to him with a huge smile on her beautiful face.

"The vacation grew on you, huh Sandra?"

"It really did. I need it," she said, staring at the box on his desk. "Case closed? What case is this?"

"Odonnell Heights shooting."

"What? When?"

"Yesterday. I got a call from the feds. Apparently, three gang members that they have in custody named Antwon Moots as the shooter."

"The same Antwon Moots that was found slain in an abandoned field? How fuckin' convenient to blame it on a dead man."

"Three gang members, same story, but are from three different parts of the city."

"It was two shooters!"

"Calm down Sandra. You're officially on vacation in six hours. A well needed vacation, enjoy it."

She sighed, turned on her Jimmy Choo heels and headed straight to the Captain's office.

Knock! Knock! Knock!
"Come in," he said. "You're not gone yet?"

"Not yet. Did you give the okay to close the Russell McGowan and Crystal Allen case, from the Odonnell Heights shooting?"

"I did. I got a call from the feds and they said three gang members identified Moots. That's why, not that I needed to give you and explanation,"

"I'm sorry captain, but there were two shooters in this case. One is still at large," she said, clearly agitated.

"The chief is on my ass about closing these unsolved murders, not yours. Again... not that I owe you an explanation," the captain said. "Forget the six hours. Go on your vacation now."

"But—"

"Now Altman! And no working any cases. If I hear about you anywhere near a case, that's you badge. Are we clear Altman?"

"Crystal," she said, pun intended.

***

Parkwood Cemetary...

Sandra drove her Audi inside the cemetery. She felt a wave of calm when she drove through the gates. She always felt relaxed when she was near Clyde Pierce... even in death.

She was so engulfed in her own thoughts, that she didn't notice riding pass George, the grounds-keeper. He got right on his phone.

She saw the fresh flowers on his grave and scowled at them.

"I'm here baby," she said, kicking the flowers away. "They didn't put them there right anyway baby." She placed the fresh flowers on his grave the way she wanted to. "Baby, they put me on forced vacation. They say I don't have a life and I be there too much." She rubbed his headstone. "Who came to see you baby? The twins? Evil-ass Tamera?"

She was there forty-five minutes later, still talking.

"I'm thinking about cutting my hair baby. I know it's long and pretty."

"Yousa disrespectful bitch, you know that?" Tammy said, startling her.

She jumped up out the grass. "I don't want no trouble, Tamera."

"Wrong! You gotta want some trouble bitch!" She spat. "You at my man's grave and—"

"Man?" she said, looking at Tammy TT Huntley. "Tammy?"

"That's right bitch," she said and hit her on her jaw. The blow was hard and staggered her.

Sandra tasted blood in her mouth. She looked at Tammy.

"What bitch? Come on, catch these hands."

"Ahhh!" she yelled and rushed Tammy.

She was rewarded with a devastating upper cut. Sandra recovered and threw two solid punches to Tammy's side and jaw. Tammy was small, but she'd been fighting for the last eighteen years. Sandra hit Tammy in her stomach, curling her up.

"Bitch!" Tammy grabbed her and beat her face repeatedly.

She was wildly swinging to get out of Tammy's grasp, to no avail.

"Bitch (punch) Clyde (punch) was never (punch) yours (punch)! Stay the (punch) fuck (punch) away from (punch) my family and (punch) this grave (punch) bitch!"

Sandra fell to the ground in a daze of confusion. Her face was a bloody mess, from the rings on Tammy's right hand.

"You just assaulted a Baltimore City Police," she said, breathlessly.

"So, try to lock me up and I'll assault you again," she said, not caring about being on parole. She had wanted to beat her ass ever since her sister told her she was harassing her sons. "Take ya broken-up-ass outta here, and take these ugly-ass flowers with you," she said, throwing her flowers.

Sandra got up and walked towards her car. "I'mma make sure you go back to jail bitch!"

"Oh, you wanna talk tough since you all the way over there? Bitch I'll come over there and beat your ass… again."

"I wish you would," she said. Sandra opened her door, grabbed her department issued 9-millimeter and held it in front of her. Tammy laughed at her "Laugh now, cry later bitch."

"Go clean ya self up, bitch. You leaking blood everywhere."

She finally pulled off. She put their flowers back in place, the way Tamera put them, and got back in the Porsche.

"You beat her ass Momma TT."

"As I should've. That bitch is disrespectful."

"She had a badge too."

"She's a police officer."

"Oh yousa gangsta Momma TT."

"That ain't gangsta chile, that's me. Now take me to see my hating-ass parole officer.

***

Half hour later, Tammy was sitting in front of her parole officer.

"Hello Ms. Huntley."

"Hi Miss Hodges."

"Any trouble?"

She thought about the money she was about to get from the dope game. "No. No trouble."

"Any new arrest?'

"No."

"Any contact with the police?"

Tammy burst in laughter until tears poured from her eyes. "I'm sorry," she said, almost feeling her knuckles connect with Sandra's face.

"Is something funny Ms. Huntley?"

"No. I was thinking of a recent event. No, no contact with the police."

"Still working at Sister's Haven?"

"Yes."

"No address change?"

"No."

"Congratulations. Your request for a transfer was okay'd. You report on Madison and Ellwood Streets next week. Stay out of trouble."

"Thank you and I will."

She walked out of Parole & Probation a very happy woman.

"Are we celebrating tonight?" Ivyana asked.

"AT! AT!" a boy yelled from a car sitting out front. The handsome boy got out of the Mercedes and approached them. "What'chu doing up here? Look, I know our last conversation ain't go too well, but I want you to know I still got ya'll back. You and my brothers," he said, temperature checking.

"London Junior, huh?"

"Yeah AT, it's me."

She got up close on him. "I'm not AT. I'm TT."

London Junior backed up some. He looked at her. He knew and saw that AT was crazy, but something gave him the eerie feeling that his father's words were true about TT. He backed all the way up to his car and got back in it.

"See you later," she mouthed towards him and walked off, with Ivyana bringing up the rear.

Chapter 9

Saturday...

Tammy, Tamera, and Ivyana was all dressed alike. Black Seven jeans and a black t-shirt with Hondo's face on it.

"I'm warning ya'll, these games get crazy."

"Tamera, I'm crazy too."

"I know you are, so am I," she said, holding up a palm size P250 9mm with a laser attachment on it.

"What'chu need with a laser Tamera?"

"My eye sight ain't what it use to be," she said, making them laugh.

"You silly."

Tammy's phone rung.

"Hello."

"Momma, where you at?"

"Over your aunt house getting ready. Why? You good?"

"No, um not good."

"What's up?" she asked, walking in the kitchen.

"I can't tell Hondo about this girl."

"Well, I figured you didn't tell him, when she called and offered to take me to see my PO."

"Momma," Honcho said, "he is gonna propose to her tonight at dinner."

"What?"

"He really love her Momma. I can't destroy this for him. I won't."

"I don't blame you. I like her, despite the lying," she said. "I mean, what was it, a few smacks and a few punches. Sauce acting all soft over that bullshit. I'll talk to him. He coming to the game?"

"No, he ain't coming," he said. "Aye Momma, be careful at the game."

"Ya'll be careful too."

"Everything okay Tammy?"

"Yeah. Ya'll ready?"

***

Later on...

Hondo warmed up, happy to be free of the colostomy bag. He felt good as he put his shots up. Hondo was in such a zone that he didn't notice that everyone had stopped what they were doing to watch him.

His shots were falling. He hit eighty-seven shots straight, nothing but net, before he missed one.

Civil came over and tapped him. Hondo removed his Beats off his head.

"What's up?'

"You warmed up yet?"

"Why?"

"Why? Hondo, you just hit eighty-seven shots straight. If you do that when the Atlanta guys get here, they won't want to bet us."

"I see." Hondo smiled. "They're here." He pointed to the entrance.

The gym's crowd swelled in a matter of minutes. The gym was standing room only.

"Come on, let them warm up," Civil said.

Hondo scanned the gym. He needed to know where all his peoples was. His mother, aunt, and girl was on the bleachers closest to the exit. Honcho and K was on the opposite side standing by the bleachers with the blue cooler. They had Jamaican J outside in the old school Cutlass with the heavy artillery. He noticed some gray bandanna wearing gang members on his mother's side of the bleachers. Which wouldn't have been such a bad thing if there wasn't some green bandanna wearing gang members on his brother's side of the bleachers. These same two gangs' deadly war began at Twon's funeral.

Hondo locked eyes with Honcho. As if sending an telepathic message, Honcho nodded letting his brother know he saw them too.

You'd think these stupid ma'fuckas would lay low with them indictments still coming down."

"K them idiots don't got common sense. They wanna be seen," Honcho said.

"Anybody like the Baltimore team for some money?" someone walked by and said with a down south accent.

"I like'em," K said. "How much you got?"

"Make it light on ya self play boy."

"You got ah thousand on you?"

"Ah band?" the country boy laughed, with a mouthful of golds.

"Make it ten bands… play boy," Honcho stepped up and said.

"I got five bands. I don't have ten."

"You confident in your boys?" Honcho asked.

"Hell yeah."

"Aiight, I'll put up ten bands, you put up that Oyster Perpetual Submariner and the five bands."

"This Rolly cost seven, play boy."

"Bullshit. What'chu think I'm dumb? That shit fifty-one seventy-five. You probably paid five on the nose nigga. Come up off that shit or beat'cha feet."

"Alright play boy," he said. "By the way, the name is Gator."

"Honcho," he said, shaking his hand.

"I knew that was you," a woman walked up and said. "It's me Mirra."

"Ohhh, I remember you. You was at the game I went to a few months back."

"That's me. I know you ain't forget all this ass. I came just because I heard your brother was playing and I know you'd be here. You gon' take my number this time?"

"Yeah, I can't promise you that threesome you want with my brother and me, but I'll be of service to ya sexy ass," he said, getting her number.

"Don't worry," she said, sucking on a red lollipop, "I'll change his mind." She walked away and all eyes was glued on her ass.

"I need to move to Baltimore." Gator smiled.

The whistle blew for the game to begin. The Atlanta boys set the tone of the game with a hard dunk the first play of the game.

Hondo was definitely not looking like himself. It was as if he turned his jumper switch off when the game started, because he couldn't hit nothing and he was getting frustrated. The five-foot-six guy from Atlanta had the clamps on him. Hondo couldn't do anything. His team had faith in him, so they kept encouraging him to shoot; nothing was falling though.

No one was more happy than Gator. His gold teeth was showing the whole time.

Half time came. Hondo's team was down by twenty-four points. Honcho walked across the court to talk to his brother.

"Lemme holla at'chu real quick bro."

"I dont' know what the fuck wrong with me bro. I can't hit shit," he said, walking away from his team.

"Ain't shit wrong with you," Honcho told him. "Take a breath, stop trying so hard. Your game is natural. I know you got a lot on ya mind right now and you got Momma, AT, and ya wifey over there. Clear ya mind. None of that matters now. The game does. That lil nigga sticking you ain't shit. Cross his ass up and do ya thing bro."

"Aiight bro."

"Let's go!"

"Hondo! Hondo! Hondo! Hondo!" Mirra and her girls chanted when Hondo walked on the court for the second half.

Civil threw the ball inbounds to Hondo, he got it stolen and the guy dunked the ball.

"Come on Hondo!" he heard Ivyana yell.

"Get your head in the game Hondo," Civil said and passed him the ball again.

The 'on' switch was flipped on and it was the Hondo show. He made his defender fall, looked at him on the floor and launched a three deep from behind the arch. The next play he crossed him up so bad the defender sprained his ankle. His replacement was treated worse. Hondo was on one.

"Where those gold teeth at Gator?" Hondo asked, when the game was over.

Gator handed over the five thousand dollars and his Rolex and walked away.

Hondo gave K three thousand dollars and turned his focus on the gang members that was now moving real fast out the gym.

"Come on K. We gotta get to my family."

After the women were safely in the car and on their way out of the parking lot K and Honcho went back to the gym to get Hondo, who had to shower and change clothes.

Mirra and two of her girls was outside the locker room waiting on Hondo.

"Honcho," Mirra sung.

"What's up?"

"Everything you can't see right now," she shot back.

Honcho just shook his head. "You tryna get the shit fucked outta you huh?"

"Yup," she said, "by you and your brother."

Hondo came out the locker room. He dapped K and his brother up. "Mirra, Kirra, Sunny, what's up?"

"You." He just laughed.

"Here bro."

"Rolly huh. Oyster."

"Take this too," he said, handing him his .45. "Twelve outside fuckin' with the gang niggas, so we going out with the girls."

"We going with ya'll tonight?"

"We got somewhere to be tonight, but I can meet up with ya'll later on."

"What about you Hondo?"

"I'm not making no promises."

"K, get some rooms, get some drinks and whatever else they want and I'll meet you and Jamaican J there later."

"Aiight."

When they walked out the doors four gray wearing gang members was waiting for them." Ya'll thought ya'll was gonna get away with killing Twon."

"Ya'll bitches get the fuck outta here."

The girls scurried off. They looked past the gang members, looking for Jamaican J. He was nowhere in sight. They did see some guys in green creeping up on them. One put his hands to his lips.

"What'chall gon' do? Twon gone."

"Oh, you tough right. You bullet proof?"

Bock! Bock! Bock! Bock!
Boom! Boom! Boom! Boom!

Chapter 10

Woodberry Kitchen Restaurant...
The women sat at the table, waiting for the men, so they could order. Tammy looked over at Ivyana.
"What's up Momma TT?"
"Ivyana, don't hurt my baby."
"Momma TT, I assure you, I got your son's best interest. I got him."
"We love those boys," Tamera added. "We don't want to see them hurt in no type of way."
"And you positive you didn't kidnap or have anything to do with the kidnapping of—"
"No Momma TT. I wouldn't lie to you or Hondo, or none of you."
"Okay."
"Bout time," Tamera said, when she laid eyes on her "handsome" nephews.
The boys kissed all the women.
"The hell took ya'll so long?"
Hondo told them the story and how the green gang snuck up and killed all four of the gang members, allowing them to get away.
"It's too many of them to ever end."
"It's gonna end, trust me," Tammy said.
They finally ordered their food. They were thirty minutes into eating when Hondo left the table. Honcho kicked his mother under the table. She excused herself as well.

Tammy found her son pacing by the bathroom.

"Son, is you alright?"

"Honcho told you?"

"You two never been able to keep nothing from me. Even me being in prison for eighteen years couldn't stop ya'll. So talk to me."

"I don't know how to do this Momma."

"I'm no expert either, but all you gotta do is be honest. Tell her how you feel and ask her the question."

"What if she say no Momma."

"Then she'd be a fool," she said. "I wanna ask you this. Are you ready?"

"You don't think I'm ready?"

"Hondo, only you know the answer to that. What I'm saying is, very soon, we are about to upset a lot of people. War is imminent son. This is why I ask are you ready. What we have planned will make everyone fair game. Can you go to war and protect your fiance?'

"Our family ain't regular Momma."

"That I know son," she smiled.

"I'm ready."

"Then go out there and claim your woman."

Tammy went back to sit down and gave her son a discreet head nod.

Hondo came back two minutes later looking more confident then ever.

"Aye, listen up ya'll. I got something to say. "Everyone stopped eating. "Bare with me 'cause this my first time, hopefully it'll be my last time." He looked down at Ivyana. "I don't know what it was about you the first night I laid eyes on you at BWX. But I knew it was something. That something made me fall in love. That something makes me want to spend the rest of my life with you." He pulled the box out, that held the ten thousand dollar engagement ring. "Do you wanna spend the rest of your life with me?"

Tears ran down her flawless face. She stood up and said, "Yes, of course, why wouldn't I. I love you Hondo!"

"She said 'yes'!" Hondo yelled, causing the who restaurant to clap.

The whole family stood up and hugged one another.

***

Two days later the wheels was in motion for their assault to begin. Ivyana was considered family so she was let in on the full scale details of their plan, and she was 100% with it.

There was only one problem.

AT's home…

They sat in front of a cache of guns, working out the minor details of their plan.

"AT, you the truth."

"I know Sauce," Tamera said.

"Let me talk to Sauce ya'll," Tammy said. The twins and Tamera walked upstairs.

"What's up Momma TT?"

"I wanted to talk to you about Ivyana." He sighed. "Come Sauce, let that go for us. She is family now."

"I can't."

"She didn't shoot you, or leave a mark on you."

"It's deeper than that TT. She put her hands on me and had me for two weeks shittin' and pissin' on myself. Two weeks."

"Sauce, how are we to go on knowing you wish to bring harm to someone in our family? A family that you belong to too."

"I don't know."

"What will it take for you to drop this? An apology? Money? Because anything physical I'm totally against."

Sauce thought about it. She had told everyone she didn't kidnap him, so if she agreed to apologize, then everyone would know she's a liar and she'd be cut off, leaving her all to him.

"Okay, I'll let it go for the sake of the family, but she gotta apologize for what she did to me."

Tammy knew what he was doing. It wasn't gonna go good, she knew. "Okay. Come on."

When they got upstairs, everyone was at the dining room table with their guns, ready to roll out. Ivyana was there as well. She held her gun tight. Sauce felt uncomfortable without a gun.

"I talked to him and he willing to let it go if Ivyana apologize."

Everyone looked at Ivyana.

"Listen, no disrespect to no one standing in this room, Sauce included, but I'm not saying this no more after this. I didn't have nothing to do with your kidnapping. I'm not apologizing for something I didn't do. It's not happening."

Tammy looked at Honcho, hoping he'd come out with what the bouncer told him. Honcho looked away from her. She shrugged, choosing to ride with her sons.

"So now what?" Sauce asked. "Twenty-five years of friendship or her?"

"Come on Sauce," Hondo said. "You going too far with this shit."

"Yo, I know what the fuck I heard."

"Aiight, so what nigga. Even if she did, you mad and wanna kill her over a few pussy ass slaps and a few punches? You geekin' nigga."

"Fuck you nigga!"

The whole family moved.

"Damn," Sauce laughed, "It's like that."

"You ain't just meet us Sauce," Hondo said. "You know how we are about family."

"Yeah, I know," he said, looking at Ivyana. "Ya'll be good... Or simply be good at it. Later." And with that Sauce was gone.

Honcho pulled Hondo to the side.
"What's up bro?"

"Hondo, I love you. I'll never go against you for any living soul. I just wanna make sure you know what'chu doing."

"You think I'm wrong."

"I didn't say that. I just wanna make sure you sure. What if Ivyana ain't being truthful bro? What if we threw away a life long friendship for a liar?"

"You don't believe her?"

Honcho sighed. "No, I don't, but I love you. So what I believe don't matter. What Pops use to tell us?"

"Right, wrong, indifferent," Hondo said.

"Aiight then nigga, act like it. We'll get Sauce back on the team."

"Get ya'll asses up here! Let's go!" They heard their aunt yell.

"Time to get this show on the road."

Chapter 11

Landry walked in the lounge all smiles. He finally got his hooks in a pretty young thing. He lived for young pussy and paid whatever he had to to keep his cravings plentiful.

When he laid eyes on Chiquetta he couldn't help but lick his lips. She looked delectable in her one piece Versace outfit and Versace heels.

"Hello pretty lady. I didn't keep you waiting long did I?'
"No. I just got here."

Landry couldn't contain his lust, it was seeping through his pores. It made her skin crawl.

"Good, can I get you something to drink?"
"Sure. Double shot of Hennessy."
"My kind of girl."

Landry went to the bar, ordered two drinks and brung them back to the table.

She downed the drink before the glass touched the table. He followed suit.

"You never told me your relationship to my nephew. You just said you looked out for him while he was locked up?" he asked, hoping she wasn't in love with him.

"I'm sorry. I lied about that."

"Huh?" he questioned.

"I said I lied. I didn't take care of him while he was locked up. I don't even know him, but we are connected.

Landry arms began sweating and sweat beads appeared on his forehead.

"I don't understand. It's getting hot as shit in here."

"I was at the funeral because of you. It was you I wanted here, now, right here in this bar."

"Huh," he said. He didn't know what was happening. His head was spinning, his vision was blurry, and he couldn't feel a thing. Then it got dark. He fell out the chair on to the floor.

"Delvon, lock up," Tamera said, coming from the back.

He hopped over the bar, locked the door and dragged Landry down to the basement where Tammy was.

An hour later they were still waiting for him to wake up.

"Delvon, you might've gave him to much."

"I gave him enough AT, chill out."

"Don't tell my sister to chill out nigga. You chill out."

"Still the same ole TT. Ya mean-ass hasn't changed one bit."

"So what."

Delvon ignored her and checked the zip ties on Landry.

"He's not going nowhere," Ivyana assured them.

Tammy made a mental note to sit down and force Ivyana to tell the story of her upbringing, because she was too calm and too skilled at this kind of work to be as innocent as her son believed. She could tell her twin sister was thinking the same thing.

Landry started moaning under the head wrap that covered his face.

"Where am I?!" Landry yelled. "Chiquetta? Where are you? Who are you? I can hear you breathing."

They removed the head wrap. He looked around the basement.

"Aww shit," he said, locking eyes with the twins, "it's two of ya'll?"

"So you know us?" Tammy asked.

"I know one of ya'll, but I thought the one was in prison."

"Thank God for parole."

"Listen ya'll, that shit was a long time ago and I ain't kill nobody," he pleaded.

"You wanted to, but the other guy pulled you out my house mother fucker."

"Who was the other guy?"

"I'm sure if ya'll found little ole me, then ya'll got to know London masterminded the whole play. Me and my brother didn't know ya'll. He told us it would be three hundred thousand a piece for us. We hopped straight on the lick. I found out years later that he wanted to rob ya'll on some jealous shit. I lost my brother that day."

"You could've said no," Tammy said.

"I could've, but I owed London from when we was in prison. He kept them gang niggas off me.

"When was this?"

"Eighty-seven was when I was in prison."

Tammy and Tamera looked at one another.

"What'chall gon' do with me? I ain't no threat to no one."

Waverly Apartments...

Gia was leaning inside the Honda, flirting with the twins, while they waited for her baby father to come back.

"Head Honcho, you been ducking me."

"No, I haven't. I know you heard about me gettin' shot."

"I did. I came up the hospital but didn't get far with the name Head Honcho. I know you miss this pussy," she said, looking at Hondo. "How I know you Head Honcho and not Hondo?"

(Laughs) "You don't know," Hondo said.

"Turn around, let us see that ass Gia." She stood up out the car window, turned around and lifted her house coat up.

"Damn, she phat as shit," Hondo said.

"Pull it down." She listened to Honcho and pulled her legging down. She didn't have on any panties, so all they saw was a perfectly, plumped, heart-shaped ass. She shook it, so they could see that it was all hers.

"There go Big Day Day," Hondo announced.

Gia didn't budge. "Ya'll done watching?" she asked with her ass still out.

"Yeah. I'mma come get you tonight. We gon' get a room."

"Both of ya'll?" she asked, pulling her leggings up.

"Take ya freak ass in the house."

"Fuck you Day Day. Bye ya'll." She waved and left.

"What'chu got Day Day?"

"Tonto's birthday is tonight. They all 'pose to be going up Melba's.

"That ain't['t gon' work. It's gonna be too many people up there with guns."

"Honcho's right. We need to get him before or after the party."

"You know his baby mother?" Hondo asked.

"Who don't' know Sasha grimey ass?"

"He still fuckin' with her?"

"He loves her from what I hear," Day Day said.

"She love him?" Honcho asked.

"She love money."

"Would she set him up for some bread?"

"I 'on't know about that. She cruddy, but I' on't know if she that cruddy."

"I know where she hang at," Hondo said. "She tried to get me to fuck her a few times."

"Aiight, good lookin' out Day Day."

"Aiight Twins."

The twins pulled off with a plan in mind.

Mc Elderry & East Avenue...

"Girl ain't nobody worried about Tavon's broke ass," Sasha said. "Money make my pussy wet."

"That's right girl," Nekita said. "These niggas be falling in love an' shit. I need that bag!"

"Lady, pass that blunt," Sherrie said.

"Sherrie, you was over there texting Sam's black-ass."

"What'cha mouth bitch."

"Yuh got weed ere?"

The females all looked at the young Jamaican and his bald friend like they were aliens. Sasha gave them the look of disgust.

"Yeah, the weed. Who got it?" K asked.

"We understood what the fuck he said. We ain't slow," Sherrie barked.

"Bitch, who got the weed?"

"Oh, this nigga tough." Sasha said, noticing the green bandanna in K's pocket. "You in the wrong neighborhood ain't'chu?"

"Bitch, my heart bleed green and my gun slump gray." K ran up on them and smack Sasha then spit on her. "I go anywhere I want bitch. Tell ya punk-ass niggas that's reppin' that bullshit-ass gray that Young Lord did it. Them pussies know how I give it up."

K went to walk off and stopped. Jamaican J knew what he was about to do.

"Matter fact," K said, "Kick all that shit out," he said.

"Please don't rob us," Sherrie pleaded.

"Oh, this bitch soft now," K laughed. "Strip bitches. Take all that shit off." K waved the FNH over the women. He took the blunt from Sherrie and began smoking on it, while they emptied their pockets, bags, and took their clothes off.

They stopped when they got to their bra and panties.

"Every-fucking-thing. And ya'll can thank ya'll tough-ass home girl." K looked at Sasha's phat ass. "Yo tough-ass phat as shit."

K and Jamaican J took all of their stuff and walked away.

The four women ran inside Sherrie's house, naked as the day they were born, crying.

"His bitch-ass gonna die," Sasha said, ran upstairs, and grabbed the house phone. She was shaking so bad, she couldn't hold the phone. "Oh God, help me," she cried.

"What's up Sasha?" he answered.

She was crying and yelling so loud, he couldn't understand her. He hung up. Sasha got her shit together and went back downstairs with her friends.

She looked around. "Where Lady go at ya'll?"

"Skumma picked her up."

She left naked?"

"Yup. What did ya baby father say?"

"Ya'll bitches go upstairs and put some clothes on and don't touch none of my new shit," Sherrie said.

They were all coming downstairs when they heard someone hitting their horn. They looked out the window and saw a Mercedes Benz AMG GTS sitting idle in front of the house. They poured out the house.

All three of them approached the car and was giving their account of what happened.

"Wait! Wait! Wait a fuckin' minute! I can't understand all ya'll at one time. Now, this nigga Young Lord robbed ya'll, stripped ya'll and said fuck the gang?"

"Yeah," they said in unison.

"And you sure he had on a green bandana?"

"Positive."

A dirt bike zoomed by too close for comfort. "What the fuck?"

The guy on the passenger side got out and looked at London Junior. "Yo, these niggas real disrespectful Down Da Hill. Let's get to this party cuz."

"Hold up homie. I gotta make sure my baby mother straight."

He got back in the car shaking his head. Mike Mike hated Sasha and hated even more, his right hand man put a baby in her. It wasn't a secret that she was a grimey hoe, but London Junior didn't care. He came when she called.

The dirt bike zoomed up again, but this time it stopped in front of them. The rider was covered from head to toe, shielding his identity.

The rider pulled out a Tech .9 and riddled London Junior's neck and face with bullets. Mike Mike jumped out with his guns and was rewarded for his bravery with a few bullets from the Tech 9 as well. The rider threw a green bandana on London's dead body and peeled off.

The girls stood frozen in shock as their eyes locked in on London Junior's body go in a spasmodic episode. When he stopped moving they knew he had transcended in to the next life.

"Bitch (cough) you (cough, cough) set us (cough) up," Mike Mike said, aiming his words at Sasha.

She turned around and looked at Mike Mike. He was bleeding from his mouth, face, and neck.

"Get (cough, cough, cough) my gun."

She didn't move. Sherrie and Nekita was too scared to move.

The sirens was getting closer. The police pulled up and that's when Sasha lost it. She screamed until she passed out.

Chapter 12

(The next day)
Division Of Corrections…

London walked out of DOC and took a deep breath and exhaled. He prayed that he never had to go to prison again.

"Where is London Junior?" he said to himself.

He waited twenty minutes. Once he didn't show up, he caught a hack to his son's house. When he got there his son's Benz wasn't in the driveway, which pissed him off more.

"Come on London. You know I got shit to do." He sat down on the steps, angry at his son.

A Crown victoria pulled up in front of the house an hour later. He figured one of the white neighbors called the police on him. When they got out with suits on, he figured the feds were there to arrest him for violation of the federal racketeering influence corrupt organization act; aka The RICO Act.

"Do you live here?"

"Why," London asked and stood up.

They looked at one another.

"Is anyone home?"

"Apparently not."

"What's your name sir?"

"London Grundy."

They looked at one another again.

"Sir, your son London Grundy Junior was found dead ten pm last night. We need someone to identify the body."

London dropped down on the steps. "No no, no, no. Fuck no! Not my boy!"

The polices allowed him to mourn. Once he got himself together, they took him to identify the body.

***

AT's home...
"What are you doing sister?"
"Tryna sharpen my computer skills," she said, typing away.
Tamera looked at the screen. "Looks to me like you house shopping."
"I'm doing that too Tamera."
"I got this big house Tammy. Why won't you just stay here? Haven't you spent enough time away from me?"
Tammy knew her sister didn't want her to go, but there was nothing like having your own. And Hondo gave her his seventy thousand dollar winnings from the basketball game towards her new home.
She stood up from the computer and hugged her sister.
"And don't keep no more secrets from me. I should've known that Hondo killed Antwoon Moots and you went to jail for the murder."
"I understand what you saying sis and I was wrong to keep that from you. But it wouldn't have made a difference. I wasn't letting my baby go to prison."
"I know, I just don't' wanna be left out like that again."
"You won't and I'm sorry."
Tammy's phone rung. She looked at it and saw Hondo's face.
"Hey baby."
"I went to Pete Cycles last night Momma."
"Did you buy the dirt bike you wanted so badly baby?"
"Yeah, I got it. It rode smooth too."
"Good, good. Well, be careful son. The streets is gonna be slippery when it rains."
"I know Momma. I love you."

"Love you more baby," she said and hung up. "That was Hondo, they got London Junior."

"Umph," Tamera said.

"AT, look, I know that kid was like a son to you, but he had to go."

"I know he had to go, but it still stings a little," she said, walked off to her room to cry.

Chapter 13

London Senior opened the door to his son's house and just stood there. He was hesitant about crossing the threshold. It didn't feel right. London Junior supposed to been showing him around the big house. He was proud of his son and his accomplishments over the past five years. He had plans to show him how proud he was of him, but now he'd never get the chance. Someone had stole that from him, and now that someone had to pay.

He walked in and closed the door. He walked over to the bar his son had built and placed the items the police gave him on the counter. London Junior's phones, money, and keys was all that was left of him. He cried looking at the items.

An hour later, he was sitting on his son's bed fresh out the shower with a towel wrappered around him.

He heard someone walking up the step. With no weapons in sight, he took the high road. A tall, brown-skin, buxom woman walked in the room with three Louis Vuitton luggage cases. She was a mess, crying, but still moving around.

London saw her from the closet, he put on a shirt and pair of pants and came out the closet.

"Shit!" she yelled. "Who the fuck… London Senior?'

"Yeah. Who are you?"

"Qutyra, London Juniors fiance," she cried." I was coming to get my things."

London sighed. "Can we talk?"

"Yes."

"Okay, meet me downstairs. Let me finish getting dressed."

London was properly dressed in an outfit that his son apparently bought for him. He found the clothes in a bag, with forty thousand in cash, a brand new iPhone and a Glock .40.

"What happened last night Qutyra?"

"We was suppose to be on our way to a party for Tonto. We were leaving when he got a call from that trifling bitch Sasha. She was screaming and crying. I don't know what was said. I just know he told me to go to the party and he'd meet me there. He never made it.

"Sasha huh?"

"Yeah, that bitch know what happened. She always in some shit with some niggas and then end up calling London. I told him to stop going when she call. I told him!"

"He went alone?'

"'He's never alone. He had Mike Mike with him. That's who called me and told me that London was dead. He got shot too."

"Where is he?"

"He might be down Central Bookings. They found two guns on him," she said. "Let me go with you to see Sasha. I'mma kick her fuckin' ass. I have that snake bitch."

"Let me go see her first. If she need to be touched, I'll let you touch her before I kill her."

She nodded. "London Junior's safe is in the basement. His money is at the top, your money that he was holding is at the bottom. I'll program my number and the safe's code in your phone." She grabbed his phone, put it in, and went upstairs to pack.

London went downstairs in the basement. The safe sat in the back of the basement behind another wardrobe. He punched the code in and opened the safe. He couldn't do nothing but cry when he seen all the money. He knew, once he seen his son's healthy kitty, that he raised a solid hustler. The tears was because he'd never get to tell his only child that he was proud of him.

London stayed in the basement for an hour thinking about his son. Qutyra was gone when he emerged from the basement. He knew he had to mentally be right before he left out the door, so he shook off the grief, and let vengeance seep into his blood stream. That was a feeling he was use to and could function with.

He grabbed the phones, his son's True Religion leather coat and the keys to the Benz.

His thoughts ran wild as he drove to his old friend's house. London knew he'd need someone he could trust on the journey he was about to embark on.

His son's Galaxy phone rung."

"Yo, man, niggas think you dead!"

London looked at the phone, the number wasn't programmed in. "Who this?"

The caller hesitated, "Who you?" he shot back.

"This London. Who's this?"

"This don't sound like London. Who the fuck are you?"

"I just told your silly-ass who it is."

"London Senior?"

"Yeah."

"You home?"

"Who the fuck is this?"

"Maniac, big bro."

London knew exactly who it was. It was Maniac, the other half of the catastrophe out Odonnell Heights, that left Eeyore and Crystal dead and the twins in the hospital.

"What's up? I thought you were gone?"

"I am. I heard London Junior got killed. That shit all on IG. Is it true?"

"Yeah, he got killed last night."

"Fuck! I'm coming back. I'll see you when I touch down," he said and hung up.

***

She hugged him when she opened the door and saw who it was.

"When did you get out?"

"This morning."

"Sorry for your lost London. That London was a sweet boy."

"Thank - you." Is Crack around?'

"I haven't seen him since yesterday morning. He probably got a new young girl. He stays out for days."

"What's his number?" She gave it to him. He called him… to no avail. "Kendra, if you hear from him, let me know. Tell'em to call me as soon as possible; it's some money in it for him."

"He'll call you for the money. You can count on it."

"Okay. I'll call you this week once I get the funeral stuff together."

"Do that London and please, stay out of trouble," she said and kissed his cheek.

"You know I'm not gonna stay out of trouble Kendra."

She smiled and watched him go.

***

Going through his son's phones he was able to find Sasha's number. London was about to call her from his phone, but stopped dialing when he thought about the possibility of having to murder her, so he called from his son's phone.

"Hello. Who is this calling from my baby father's phone."

"This London."

"Stop fuckin' playin'. Who the—"

"It's London Senior, Sasha. Where you at?" I need to see you."

"Poppa London? When did you get out?"

"This morning. Where are you?"

"Down my home girl's house, where it happened at. Down Da Hill on McElderry and East Street. First house on the corner."

"Stay put. I'm on my way."

He pulled off, hoping he could keep his cool around the conniving woman.

Sasha was standing on the porch in some too small shorts and a t-shirt that barely covered her breast in November. Two more girls appeared once the Benz came to a stop.

London got out. Three guys came out the house. He could tell they strapped.

"Sasha, let's talk," London said.

"Yo Sasha. When you gon' be done?"

She turned around. "Nigga this is London's father. Have some fuckin' respect!"

The guys posture changed up quick. London threw up a gang sign, the guys threw one up back as a sign of respect.

They got in the car.

"Tell me what happened, and not the version you gave the police."

She gave him the story how it happened, minus Mike Mike's accusation of her involvement.

"The green huh? Them stupid niggas killed my boy? Them broke-ass dirty niggas," he fumed. "On the other hand, my son would still be alive, had you not called him?"

She couldn't answer him.

"I know you said something slick to the nigga. You left that part out. But it doesn't matter. I'm going to find the bald head guy and this fuckin' Jamaican and kill them and the their next of kin. And do me a favor."

"Anything Poppa London."

"Stop saying my son is your daughter's father, 'cause we both know that ain't true. He told me about the blood test. It's time for you to live off of your own name and on your own two."

"Okay," was all she could say.

"I know you said you don't know the two guys, but where is the closest green hood to here?'

"Highland Town. They be up on Leverton."

"Aiight. You may wanna go home and stay from around here, because shit about to be hot around here."

"Okay." She got out of the Benz feeling naked. She no longer had the protection of the gray gang. She knew she'd have to slow down.

She walked up the steps looking stupid. London called the three guys over to him. He spoke to them for a few minutes. After he was done, they walked away. They didn't go back to Sherrie's house. They didn't even look Sasha's way.

Sasha knew it was over then. She sighed and shook her head.

Chapter 14

For twenty-five minutes Hondo had been without his eye sight. He had no idea what his girl had planned, but he was trusting her. All he knew was, she pulled up in a all white S600 Mercedes Benz, with a blindfold in her hand and asked him, "Do you trust me?" with the blindfold raised in the air. He did trust her, but he wasn't sure and his senses was going haywire. He still elected to trust her. But she wasn't making it no better by not saying a word the whole drive.

They came to a complete stop forty-five minutes later. She led him up some steps and through a door.

She removed the blindfold. He looked around, admiring the de'cor of the beautiful home, that he assumed was hers, since he was always asking to go to her home.

He grabbed her and tried to bring her in for a kiss. "Slow down, horny boy."

She pushed him away.

"So this is where you live, huh?" He said, walking around.

"I never knew my father," she began. "And I only heard about my mother. I grew up with a lady that my mother knew. Not one of her family members, a woman she knew. A woman that was a recovering addict. That's how me and my sister grew up."

"The pretty girls that wore dirty clothes and dirty shoes. In two thousand -five at twelve years old we had enough. So we started hustling."

"At twelve?"

"Twelve."

"I can't talk, me and Honcho started working for AT at ten. We were baggin' up at eight."

"Can I finish?"

He seen the seriousness in her. She wanted to tell him her story; the mystery he always said surrounded her. "By all means," he said and sat down on the couch.

"Anyway, we were natural hustlers and we enjoyed doing it. The lady we were staying with was fed up with us and was ready to put us away. She claim she went to our mother complaining about our behavior and our mother financed our relocation here in DC. I didn't believe that shit. My sister didn't either. But we rolled with it. We did the same shit here, we did in Baltimore. We finished school and did two years of college and that was it. We wanted to be in the streets. So we been in them."

"The end?"

"Thee end," she answered. "Got any questions, sir?"

"Sir?" he questioned and laughed. He thought about what she just laid in his lap. It didn't take a rocket scientist to figure out that his girl was from the streets. She didn't scare easy, and she was always down with a mission. She was the best of both worlds.

"Think hard."

"You ever think about your mother?"

"Some times."

"You ever thought about finding her?"

"Once. Me and my sister wanted to look for her, but the lady scared us out of doing so."

"How?"

"She said that if we opened up that door we wouldn't like what we found and we'd be separated," she said. "The word separated, alone, was enough to get us to forget all about the lady that gave us away."

"You and your sister seem to be tight, why I never seen her?"

"But you have," she said. "She's sitting right in front of you."

It hit him just then; like a ton of bricks. He knew what was wrong with her. She was sexy, her breath or feet didn't stink, her toes was pretty and her box stayed fresh, but he figured out her flaw: She was crazy. Mentally messed up from a screwed up childhood. She was bipolar, schizophrenic, she hallucinated, and had multiple personalities.

He shook his head.

"What?" she said.

(Sighs) "Look Ivyana, I can get you some help."

She laughed uncontrollably for five minutes straight. When she stopped laughing abruptly, she said in a weird scary movie voice, "My name isn't Ivyana... it's Iyana."

Hondo looked at her to see if she was being serious. She didn't show a hint of humor.

"You love my sister don't you?"

Hondo didn't know what to say. He was too heartbroken.

"She loves you. I can tell. She never stayed away from me until she met you. I mean never. I got locked up once for assault on a police officer, do you know she hit the paddy wagon police so we could be together up Northern District Police station. But then you came along."

"Ivyana, you need to move to Baltimore, so I can look over you."

She laughed hysterically again. "You really think I'm crazy, don't you?"

"No."

"That's your first lie."

She was right.

"Do you take medication?"

"No boy. I don't take shit. My sister don't either."

"Can we go to your bedroom?"

"Why?" she asked, with her face contorted. "I just told you I'm Iyana and you still wanna go to my bedroom?"

"I wanna go to Ivyana's bedroom," he said, playing her game.

"Come on." She got up and Hondo followed her.

When they walked up the steps, he shook his head. *All this "ass" is crazy,* he thought. He reached out to grip her phat ass but thought against it. He didn't want to have to beat her up for zapping out.

"Here is my sister's room."

"Can I go in?"

"She in there, go ahead," she said, smiling.

He opened the door and was shocked into silence. He couldn't say nothing.

"That's the look you had on your face the night we met," Ivyana said, smiling.

"You still think I'm crazy?"

He just shook his head. "Identical twins. I got gamed by the game I been using on people my whole life," he laughed.

"What's funny is you thought I was crazy."

"Ivyana and Iyana," he said.

"Ivy and Iya for short."

"Wait until I tell Honcho."

"No babe, let us get him."

"I 'on't know about that Ivyana."

"Come on, let us have some fun."

He was about to agree when something hit him. He turned to Iyana. "It was you."

"Huh?"

"You. You kidnapped Sauce."

"Okay, it was me, but I didn't hurt him and he tried to kill my sister. Honestly Hondo, if my sister didn't truly love you, Sauce would've been dead for that stunt."

"I can say the same for you too. I lost a good friend behind your shit."

"How was I suppose to know he ain't kill Malik to keep the money? Once I verified his story, I let him go. But I'm a female, I always gotta go the extra mile to let niggas know I'm not playing. Shit, I would've shot him, if Malik ain't tell me he trusted him the most out of everyone he served. He came in with the benefit of doubt. So give me that."

"I'm gonna holla at him. The time is here that we're gonna need our whole family."

"Oh, I'm family now?"

"Yeah Iyana, you family."

Chapter 15

Odonnell Heights Projects…

Sauce walked in Crystal's old house, where K, Jamaican J, Honcho, Delvon, Tammy and Tamera was already waiting.

"I told ya'll I was done," Sauce said.
"Shut up and get over here and give your AT a hug."
He smiled and went to hug Tamera.
"I ain't kissing his ass," Tammy barked. "He could've stayed gone for all I care."
"It's good to see you my man," Honcho said, dapping him up.
"Good to see you too my nigga."
"Bro hit you too?"
"Yeah, he hit me and told me to meet him here."
"Anybody tryna shoot," K asked.
"Oh he don't know, do he sis?" Tamera said, pulling money out of her Chanel bag.
"What we shootin'?"
"Make it light on you. What's your rules?"
Hondo walked in the house before the game could start. He hugged his mother and aunt and dapped everyone else up.
"Yo, I called everybody here to put'chall up on what's going on. London is home. Him and some of his gang hit the green gang up Highland town."
"That's good," Tammy said. "We can now send our message."
"Why am I here?"
"You'll be effected if it comes out we were behind London Junior murder?"

"That was ya'll?" Sauce asked.

"It don't matter if it was," Tammy said. "We gotta get our shit together. Nobody else is dying. Eeyore and Crystal was enough."

Sauce still didn't know what any of this had to do with him.

"Once our message is clear it's gonna be on."

"Why am I here?" he asked, clearly frustrated.

Hondo sent a text on his phone and in one minute, one of the twins was standing next to him. Sauce mugged her.

"Listen, I apologize for causing this confusion in ya'll family. Not to go all the way in details, but a large sum of money was owed to me and I did what I had to do to get it back, but it wasn't nothing to die over. A few slaps and punches by me, not my men, so why you still up tight Sauce?'

"You lied to me to my face," Tammy said.

"I knew it was you," Honcho said casually.

"How you know bro?"

"I didn't tell you Hondo, but I went to see the bouncer and he said Ivyana was the one who paid him the thousand dollars to feed us the fake story about a brown-skin nigga."

"I didn't lie to you Ms.Tammy," Iyana said.

Honcho sent another text out.

"But you right Honcho, it was me who paid the bitch-ass bouncer nigga."

Ivyana walked in the house and stood on Hondo's right side.

"What the fuck!" Honcho yelled.

"Ain't this ah bitch," Tamera said.

Tammy and K laughed until tears formed in their eyes.

Sauce just stared at both women.

"I never lied to any of you. Not once. But I would've, if any of you would've asked me did I know who did it; instead of did I do it. I would've had to lie to ya'll, because win, lose, draw, death, or life, I'm rockin' out with my sister."

"That's what the fuck I'm talking about," Tammy said. "Loyalty!"

"Hey everybody, my name is Iyana," she said and walked up on Sauce. "I'd be lying if I said I didn't mean what I did. Two hundred thousand is a lot of bread. I'm a woman, a pretty one at that, so everything I do gotta be extra. So where we going from here?"

Sauce wanted to punch her right in her pretty face, but he had choked her sister out and she was innocent. He had also gained some respect for the twin women. "We even."

She held out her hand and he shook it.

Chapter 16

It was certainly no funeral. It was truly a celebration. London didn't want to send his son off with everyone crying around him. He wanted everyone to enjoy his son's life like he lived his life; fun.

He rented out The Hot Spot on Guilford Avenue and threw a party. He sat up in the DJ's booth area because he didn't want everyone coming up to him offering him their condolences. He wanted everyone to enjoy themselves and leave, so he could get back to crippling the green gang.

His actions and transgressions in Highland town, against the green gang, sparked off a deadly gang war in the Maryland Prison System. Every prison in Maryland was on lockdown. There was ten fatalities and over a hundred stabbings. With the upper echelon of both gangs sitting on Madison Street at the federal Chesapeake Detention Center awaiting trial, no one was on the streets to stop the blood bath.

He seen Qutrya walk in. He was about to go meet her until someone pointed him out to her. She walked up the steps to the DJ's booth.

"What's going on?" she asked, hugging him. "You feel better? I heard about Highland Town."

"I don't feel no better Qutyra."

"Only time will heal us."

"What'chu drinking?'

"Nothing. I missed my period. I may be pregnant."

London Junior smiled. "Finally, a grandchild. I hope you are preg—"

He stopped in mid-sentence, with his eyes glued on the door. He removed his Tom Ford shades to make sure he wasn't seeing things.

London patted his side, reassuring that he was carrying. "Stay here, don't move."

"Okay," she said.

"What's up London," Maniac asked. "You good?'

"Yeah, I'm fine," he said and went to the entrance to meet a blast from his past. "What the fuck are you doing here, bitch?" Didn't I tell you I never wanted to see you again?"

"Wrong and is that any way to speak to your child's mother?'

"My son is dead, as you can see," he said, pointing to the casket on the stage, "So you dont' even fuckin' exist no more." London hated his son's mother because he loved her so much and she left him, and with her standing right in front of him, old feelings was rearing its ugly head. "Why are you hear?"

"To see my son off."

"Your son? Bitch please. He ain't been ya son in eighteen years."

"London, my name ain't bitch. That's your second time calling me out my name in three minutes. Don't let it be a third time. In case you forgot, my name is La'toya." She walked pass London, bumping his shoulder, and went straight to her son's casket.

London had him dressed in his favorite clothing brand; Versace and a pair of all white Versace shoes.

"La'toya looked at her son and shook her head. "I knew when you were born that you were gonna be a handful."

London Senior came and stood beside her.

"I always told your father that karma was real. He use to think I was crazy. I knew, felt, and understood… and eventually accepted when you were five years old, that you wouldn't live a full life."

London looked at her like she was possessed by a dark force.

"You lay here today, because of the actions of your father."

London began thinking. *What if I'm the reason my son is laying here dead? What if my actions eighteen years ago was the reason? What if La'toya was right?* That was too much to bear. He didn't want to live with that. He felt his mental slipping.

"Open your eyes London," she said, "this is your work."

London punched La'toya in her face. He didn't know that she was already unconscious, he got down on one knee and punched her some more, until he got tired.

Qutyra and another guy pulled him off of her before he caught a murder charge.

He looked at them. Everyone was looking at him. London broke free from them and ran outside. London pulled his phone out and dialed a number.

"Hello, Moots residents. May I help you?"

"Kendra, this London."

"Hey London."

"You still haven't heard from Crack?"

"No. I filed a missing persons report a few days ago. Young girl or no young girl he do not stay gone and don't call me."

"How did they find out," he said to himself.

"Who? How did they find out what?"

"I'll call you back Kendra. "He hung up the phone. He knew if the twins was behind his son's murder and Cracks disappearance, then he was next on their list. The worst part of it all, he knew that he had only himself to rely on.

***

Hondo, Honcho, Ivyana, and Iyana was driving from out the projects in a stolen Dodge Durango.

"Where we going now Honcho?"

"We going to Waverly Apartments to holla at some people."

Honcho phone rung.

"Yeah Momma."

"Did you send that text?"

"Message sent."

"Good. Where you at?"

"'Bout to go check on something real quick. We'll meet'chu at AT's house in ah hour."

"Love you."

"Love you more."

They pulled up in Gia's court and noticed a lot of guys in front of her house.

"Fuck is going on over here?"

"I'on't know Honcho."

"Who ya'll looking for? Let us go over there."

"Yeah," Ivyana said, "this is what we do."

"Aiight, look, do this…"

The guys was drinking, smoking, and passing around percocets and mollies to escape the grief of losing a fallen comrade.

It was like time froze when the women walked up on them.

"Is Gia in there?"

"Who ya'll? My name Hoffa."

"God," Ivyana said, covering her mouth and nose, "is that your breath nigga, damn."

"Come on sis." They walked in the house, where it was more guys. "Gia!" Iyana called out.

"Who calling me?"

"Damn," the twins said, when they laid eyes on the sexy, thick, half black, half Korean woman.

They looped their arms around hers and Ivyana whispered. "Honcho's outside in the parking lot waiting for you. Come on."

"Where you going Gia?"

"With my cousins real quick. I'll be back."

"Put us on Gia," one of them yelled after them.

She ignored him and let the twins guide her to Honcho.

"Hey ya'll," she said, when they all got in the truck.

Ivyana pulled off.

"You heard from DayDay?"

"Shit, it's business. I thought ya'll was coming to grant my ultimate fantasy. Getting fucked by two sets of twins. Identical at that."

"For the record, I'm the only one that fucked Gia," Honcho smiled.

"Oh, I'm sorry, no disrespect."

"It's okay Gia. You ah bad bitch. Me and Hondo may give you a call. I wouldn't mind seeing what you taste like."

"Me either," Iyana said.

Hondo and Honcho were both shocked.

"You were saying Honcho?"

"Oh shit. You heard from Day Day?"

"No, he went to London Junior's funeral slash party."

"Here," Honcho said, passing her an envelope.

"What's this?"

"Twenty-five thousand dollars. I want you to take Lor DayDay and your other son and get out of Baltimore for a few weeks."

"Okay."

"Don't play Gia. Leave. We'll call you when it's safe to come back," Honcho said.

"Okay."

***

London didn't have time to mourn his son. He was back in the trenches with the wolves and possibly at war with four cold blooded killers.

He had a million thoughts running around in his head as he eyed his son's small, but deadly, arsenal. Two Dracos, one AK-47, one SKS, two bulletproof vests, and two H&K .40s; all loaded and ready for action.

London didn't trust Maniac, so he wasn't depending on him. He had to be smart if it was AT and TT that he was up against.

He put a vest on and bagged everything else up in a Louis Vuitton duffle bag.

He had the key in the lock of the trunk when he smelled it. "What the fuck?!" He fell back on the ground of the driveway, when the trunk opened.

"Motherfucker," he fumed, getting up off the ground. He covered his nose and went back to the trunk.

Crack was in the trunk of his son's Dodge Charger, neck slit from ear to ear, with a note that read: *Family Over All Else,* in what appeared to be blood.

There was no doubt in his mind about his deep, dark secret being out in the open.

He would answer for shooting his best friend; Clyde Pierce, in the head two times. He didn't feel no way, still, about killing Hondo and Honcho's father. He wanted to be the man, and he couldn't do that with Clyde around.

He stared in the dead eyes of the man that helped him eighteen years ago.

Now that he was one hundred percent sure who he was up against, he didn't know what to do. Then his phone rung.

He answered it. Ten minutes later, the scale of war was dramatically tipped in his favor. He smiled and rubbed his hands together.

Chapter 17

The streets were awkwardly quiet. It was the calm before the storm, the police knew.

Detective Sandra Altman, who was recently deputized by the federal government, and her partner Detective James Woody sat at the table waiting for everyone to come in to be debriefed.
United States Attorney Steven Voul entered the room with Special Agent Keys and lead Agent Sanduski.
"Everyone, please, let's get started. I have a very important meeting in an hour," Voul said.
"We have enough to charge London Grundy at this point, sir."
"Why isn't he in custody then?"
The agents looked at Altman.
"Care to explain Ms. Altman?"
"Sir, I believe we can get some more players. Why stop with Grundy sir?"
"Grundy was who we were after Detective Altman."
"She believes we can also get the twins that was shot out Odonnell Heights a few months ago and their recently paroled mother and her sister.
"And what do we have on them?"
"Nothing now, SA Voul."
"Are they members of this gray gang?"
"No," Special Agent Keys said.
"Yes, they are."
All eyes went on Detective Altman.

"I gained intelligence from an informant that Honcho Pierce was protected by the gray gang while on a five year prison bid."

"Well, the gray gang doesn't protect you, unless you're affiliated," SA Voul said. "You have three days to get something on them. If you don't have them then, then you won't have them on our dime."

"Thank you.'

"Don't thank me, get to work."

"You want them that bad huh?" Woody asked when they got in the car.

"What?"

"You know what. You know got damn well Pierce rejected their protection and stabbed one of them every chance he got."

"Well, I didn't lie."

"You so hell bent on destroying this family, you're destroying yourself in the process."

"I'm fine."

"What happened to your face while you were on vacation?"

"I told you already."

"Bar fight, bullshit. You don't even drink," he said. "And how do you plan to get evidence on this family when no one has heard a peep from them in weeks. Even Grundy's wire is saying they disappeared or is hiding from him."

"Let me do this."

***

Hondo, Honcho, and their mother shut down their operations in the projects to avoid innocent people dying. They also advised everyone to stay in doors.

Hondo and Honcho rode the streets of Baltimore looking for London, while Jamaican J and Sauce did the same. K worked better alone, so he was off doing his own thing.

Gia popped in Honcho's head so he decided to go see if she really left.

"Stupid ma'fucka," Hondo said when he seen all the front room lights on in her house.

"Man, I hope this Day Day in here."

"Me too."

They got out the car and approached the house. Halfway there, they both got eerie feelings. They looked around to see if anyone was out lurking around. It looked clear, but looks were deceiving, so they both pulled out their .45's and approached cautiously.

They reached the door and seen that it was kicked in, but closed as best it could.

"Shit," Hondo whispered.

"Come on bro, we going in."

The house was in shambles. Everything that was supposed to be upright, was upturned. Everything that was suppose to be whole, was either in pieces or had a hole in it.

The twins paused and listened for movement. They heard none, so they proceeded to Lor Day Day's room. His room was in perfect condition.

Not one thing was out of place. Gia's room was a different story. All they could do was shake their heads when they saw Day Day's body.

"Damn," Honcho said.

"Come on bro, let's get outta here."

They went to the door and saw a police car pulling in the parking lot. They ran through the house and out the back door. They never even looked back.

They didn't relax until they were in the hack on their way to their hotel room.

***

2:15 am...

"Drop mi right ere bredren."

"You sure J?"

"Mi gah git fi blunts fi mi ganja smoke."

"Aiight, I'll wait for you," Sauce said.

"Mi gud," he said, holding up the Glock. 40.

"Naw J. Go get the blunts and I'll drive you in the projects."

"Mi gud," he said and got out the car.

When he came out he walked pass Sauce's car and walked towards the projects.

"Come on J, stop playin' bro. Get in the car," Sauce got out the car and said.

"Mi gud. Leave mi," he said, and kept walking.

"Weird ass nigga," Sauce said and got back in the car.

"J," Nay-Nay called out when he reached Shipview Way. "You got a cigarette?"

"Yea gal."

"Where is the twins and Sauce? They need to hurry up and get this shit over with."

Scarrrrrrd!

Jamaican J moved Nay-Nay behind him and moved his hand to his waist.

Bock! Bock! Bock! Bock! Bock! Bock!

He didn't get off one shot. Jamaican J's body hit the ground hard. Nay screamed her heart out.

Chapter 18

The Hilton Hotel...
Ivyana rolled over and grabbed the vibrating phone. She looked at the phone.
"Babe, wake up. The phone."
"Huh."
"The phone."
He grabbed it. "Yo."
"Answer the phone babe."
He hit the green button on the screen. "Yo."
"Wake up Hondo."
"I'm up K. What's up?"
"Jamaican J. He gone bro. He got caught 'round the way last night coming from Joe's Bar."
"Where was Sauce?"
"Sauce said J jumped out the car on him."
"Shit. Where you at?"
"In Nay-Nay's house. The 'jects crawling with cops. The demon bitch out here too!"
"Get with Sauce and meet me out AT's house."
Honcho and Hondo left the girls in their rooms and headed to Tamera's.
"What's up with you and Iyana, bro?"
(Laughs) "Not a damn thing, but you know I tried. She was on some other shit."
"What was she on?"
"She said she don't have casual sex and called me a lor boy."
(Laughs)

"That shit ain't funny bro.I wanted to fuck her phat ass bad as shit. Then she had the nerve to be walking around the room in some lor ass True Religion booty shorts. Them shits didn't even cover her ass cheeks bro."

"Damn," Hondo said. "You want me to say something to her?"

"Hell naw bro. I'm not ready for no commitment. That's what she want."

"Aiight."

When they pulled up to the house, Tammy was pulling out the driveway, with Delvon behind her in his car. They pulled up beside their mother and let the window down.

"What's up Momma?"

"Momma."

"Hey, my handsome men."

"Where you going?"

"Going to see my PO."

"Be careful Momma."

"I will, that's why I got Delvon," she said. "K and Sauce are in there waiting on ya'll."

"Aiight."

K was dipping in Tamera's bar when they walked in. They dapped them up.

"What the hell happened?"

"I told this crazy ass nigga not to walk to the projects. We stopped at Joe's 'cause he wanted some cigarettes. When he came out he walked across the street. I basically begged the nigga to get back in the car. He said Mi gud. So I rolled out."

"You still should've went with him Sauce," Hondo said.

"That nigga grown bro. I couldn't drag the nigga back in the car."

"What happened in the projects K?"

"Nay-Nay said she asked him for a cigarette and asked him where ya'll was at. Then a green Mazda pulled up and started shooting. She said J pulled her behind him so she wouldn't get hit."

Both twins shook their heads.

***

Madison Street & Ellwood Avenue...
Parole & Probation...

Tammy enjoyed going to see her PO at the new place because she didn't have to wait long. And her PO, Mr. Martin, was cute and cool for a white man. She liked him better than Miss Hodges. He complimented her and she believed he was sweet on her.

"Huntley!"

Tammy got up and walked in the back with the woman.

"Are you prepared to take a urine test today?"

"Yes, I am."

She submitted the urine sample and was escorted back to Mr. Martin's office.

"Hi Mr. Martin."

"Hello Ms.Huntley," he smiled. "You look nice today... as always."

"Why thank you. You don't look so bad yourself," she said, making his cheeks turn rosey red.

"Anything new?"

"No sir."

"How are your boys doing?"

"Working and being boys?"

(Laughs) "Any police contact?"

"No sir."

"Still at your sister's bar?" he asked.

"Yes. I'm still there."

"And your address is still the same?"

"Yes sir."

"Okay. I'll be doing a home visit on Monday. That's ok with you?"

"Yes. I'll take off of work that day, so I can be there… because no one else will."

"Umph," he smiled. "I'll see you next week Ms. Huntley."

"I guess you will."

"I'll walk you out. Come on," Mr. Martin said. He walked out to the front. "I'm going out to smoke a cigarette Monique."

"Okay Mr. Martin."

Mr. Martin lit up a cigarette when they got outside. "You know I got a friend that owns a huge company out in Howard County. He could use a receptionist. The benefits are amazing too."

"Why are you so good to me?"

Mr. Martin was about to answer until he saw a masked man fastly approaching them, holding a handgun, with an extended clip. He dropped the cigarette and pushed Tammy over the railing.

Bock! Bock! Bock! The gunman hit Mr. Martin high in the chest. **Bock! Bock!**

The gunman was still advancing, trying to locate his target when he heard, **Boom! Boom! Boom! Boom!** The deafening shots from the fifty caliber Desert Eagle was enough to deter the gunman from pursuing Tammy. He ran away from the scene.

Delvon ran and jumped in his car. He drove around to where he seen Tammy pushed off the landing. She was holding her arm, but she was good. The sirens could be heard.

Being excellent under pressure, he said, "You good TT. I'll be back after I get rid of the car." He pulled off at a normal speed and made a left on Monument Street.

***

Johns Hopkins Hospital… (Two Hours Later)

Two detectives sat at the foot of Tammy's hospital bed. One was taking notes and the other one was asking the questions.

"... and Ms. Huntley, you're one hundred percent sure you heard the gunman yell Mr. Martin's name before the shots?"

"Yes, I am sure," she said, with as much emotion as she could muster up. "He saved my life."

"And you didn't see the shooters at all?"

"No."

"Everyone inside of the probation place said that there was a pause before the bigger gun shots. You have any idea why that was?"

"No sir."

"Okay Ms. Huntley. I'm going to leave my card here. If you remember anything, don't hesitate to call me."

"Okay."

The detective left his card on her bed and walked out with his partner in tow.

Hondo, Honcho, and Tamera rushed in her room and showered her with affection

"Ouch, my arm is broke ya'll!" she yelled.

"Sorry Momma."

"What they saying about discharging you? We need you up outta here," Tamera asked.

"I can go now. They just gave me a room because the police wanted to see me."

The nurses wheeled another patient by them to the other half of the room. They all looked at the patient roll by.

"Damn, she fucked up."

Tamera smacked Honcho's shoulder. "Shut up boy."

"Excuse me, nurse," Tammy called out.

"Yes."

"I'm ready to go."

"Yes. They told me to process you out. We're waiting on your paper work Ms. Huntley," the nurse said and went back to getting her patient comfortable.

"You wanna talk in here?" Hondo whispered when the nurse left.

Tammy motioned for them to huddle up. "They tried to kill me today. My PO saved my life and got killed in the process."

"Where the fuck was Delvon?"

"He did what he was suppose to do, Hondo." she said.

"We can't drive no more of our cars," Tamera said.

"AT's right. We gotta put all our cars up. They know our cars."

"Tammy and Tamera."

They all looked over to the curtain that was separating the patients.

"Ya'll know her?" Honcho whispered.

They both shook their heads.

"AT and TT," the voice said

Hondo pointed at his mother and aunt and whispered, "She know ya'll."

They both shrugged. Hondo pulled the curtain back revealing the drubbed woman.

"Long time no see," the woman said. "Still don't know who I am huh?"

They looked at the woman, trying to see pass the cuts, bruises, lumps, and purple skin.

"Oh my motherfuckin' gawd," they said simultaneously.

"It can't be," Tamera said.

Chapter 19

Brooklyn Holmes Projects...

Sass walked in the house and went straight in the kitchen where London was loading a Glock .40.

"You officially a fugitive big home boy. The cops are all over ya son spot. I sent a female down the block and they swarmed her car."

"Shit, that was quick. I just missed my PO appointment yesterday."

"London, this ain't about no appointment. She said these cops was mixed, Regular polices, DEA, ATF, and FBI flaps on their jackets. This is the big leagues, big bro."

"I ain't going back to prison. Fuck that," London proclaimed. "What the fuck happend on Madison Street?"

"The stupid-ass PO got in the way and no one said she'd have someone watching her. That nigga came outta nowhere bustin' at me. I almost got hit."

"We gotta get these ma'fuckas Sass. The net is coming down one me," he said, thinking. "Drastic times calls for drastic measures. Call Maniac and tell'em I got a job for him."

***

Johns Hopkins Hospital...

Tammy and Tamera both were up and standing over top of the beaten woman.

"La'toya Mcbride."

"We thought you were dead," Tammy said.

"No, I'm not. Although London tried last week."

"What?"

"He tried to kill me at my son's funeral."

"I'm sorry to hear about London Junior. We heard about that," Tamera said.

"I got something to tell ya'll," she said. "I should've been told ya'll, but we weren't exactly friends. The cheating, the pregnacy, the physical and verbal abuse, none of that made me walk away from him, but his disloyalty was.

"I left Baltimore and him and my son, because I overheard him talking one night about a robbery he set up that he didn't make no money from and someone got killed in the process. I seen the news that morning and saw what happened in the projects. I asked him about it and he beat my ass and told me to never get in his business again.

"I knew nothing good would come from his actions, so I left."

"My sister did eighteen years in prison because of that night."

"My man; my son's father was killed that night. And London pulled the trigger."

"Don't worry, London is going to prison for a long time and I'm going to make sure of it."

"What?"

"Prison," Tammy questioned.

"Yes, he beat me at my son's funeral and this guy pulled him off me. He also brung me to the hospital."

"And."

"He ended up being an undercover federal agent. He was there watching London. They got his phone tapped and everything. I'm testifying against him."

"You gonna snitch on him?"

"Yup."

"That's some bitch shit," Tammy said.

"I'm not in the streets. I don't have a code. I'm not snitching on him to gain anything, nor am I getting anything in return."

"Snitching is snitching. I don't give ah fuck how you dress it up," Tammy said. "Leave my family's name out your mouth. Let my man continue to rest in peace."

Delvon picked them up an hour later. They knew time was of the essence. They had to get to London before the feds.

Chapter 20

Honcho's house…
Ivyana jumped up and hugged Tammy when they walked in the house.

"Momma TT!"

"Damn girl, I'm okay. I got a broken arm."

"I'm glad you're okay."

Honcho went in his basement and grabbed the large duffle bag that contained his arsenal. They had tried to kill his mother, so the gloves was off.

Hondo was at his side two minutes later. "What's next bro?"

"Hondo, we gotta get this nigga before the feds get'em. I'm not tryna let this nigga go in the system. Fuck that!"

"I'm with you. I just can't think straight with Momma and AT here. Them niggas tried to take Momma out. I want them to go to DC with Ivyana and Iyana. Shit gettin' too dangerous up here."

"Honcho, I wanna see how you gonna explain this to Tammy TT Huntley. That lady ain't going no-fuckin'-where."

"Shit!" he yelled in frustration. "Then we out here blind as fuck. With Day Day dead, we 'on't have shit."

His phone vibrated.

"Yo."

"Where ya'll at?"

"At my house, why?"

"I got something, we gotta move now though. I'm on my way," Sauce said and hung up.

"Come on bro, grab a gun. Sauce on his way to get us."

Thirty Minutes Later...
"Where we going?"

"Brooklyn. One of my bitches said her homegirl is letting London and some of those gang niggas hold up in her house."

"Fuck yeah!" Honcho yelled. "Got that ass now."

"That ain't all ya'll," Sauce said. "Maniac is in there too, and he was the one who tried to shoot TT at Parole and Probation."

"Maniac," the twins repeated, simultaneously, unconsciously rubbing their gunshot scars that they acquired by the hands of Twon and Maniac in the projects a few months ago.

"This turned out to be a beautiful day." Hondo said, anxious to get the beef over with.

Honcho's mind was on his father. He remembered the day his father was killed, vividly. His seven-year-old mind knew and felt he'd never see his father smile again. He knew his father could never give him another lesson on the importance of loyalty to his brother. His father was stolen from him, by a disloyal, jealous friend. He would pay back the debt London owed to his family.

***

Central Police Department...
Detective Sandra Altman was at her desk waiting on a call from Special Agent Keys that her boss said would be coming through any minute.

"What do you think it's about?"

"I don't know Woody," she said. "Did you know that Tammy Huntley was involved in that shooting at Parole and Probation on Madison Street?"

Woody's jaw dropped. "How so?"

"That was her parole officer and she was standing outside with him when the shooting began."

"Death follows this family like the plague.

Ring. Ring. Ring.

"I have to take this, excuse me." she said and answered the phone.

"Altman, sorry, my boss wants Grundy off the streets now."

"What? Why?"

"He's too dangerous to lay on Altman. And we have him on a murder from nineteen ninety-nine."

"Ninety-nine? Who?"

"Aahhh, Clyde William Pierce."

"What?!" she screamed. Her mind was swirling. "London killed Clyde."

"You know this Clyde?"

"No. I have to go. Thanks for calling," she said and hung up. She put her hands on her head as the missing pieces to the puzzle began connecting. The twins shooting out Odonnell Heights. London Junior death. The twins beef with the gray gang. London's release. The PO's shooting with TT there. London on the wire taps talking about killing twin boys. She put it all together.

She grabbed her bag and her personal car keys.

"Where are you going Altman?"

"Out, I'll be back."

"I'm going," Woody insisted.

She stopped dead in her tracks and turned towards him. "No, you aren't."

"You're about to do some stupid shit. I can see it in your eyes."

"I'm not about to do shit," she said and disappeared out the door.

"Shit," Woody fumed. *I'm not losing my badge for her,* he thought. He got up and walked to the captain's office.

"Can I help you James.?"

"Yes," Woody said. "I have to talk to your sir."

"I'm listening."

***

Brooklyn Holmes Projects…

They were sitting in Dantrey Court watching the house Sauce told them about.

"Why we waiting?"

"We don't know what's inside waiting for us." Sauce said.

"That's the fun part. Come on," Hondo said and got out. Honcho was right on his heels with two FNs out.

Sauce sighed and got out behind them. "These two niggas crazy," he mumbled.

"We knocking or what bro?"

"Naaaah. Let's go with the no knock-warrant," Hondo said. He raised his ACG Nike Boots and kicked the door in. "Everybody get down! ATF! ATF! Get the fuck down!"

They couldn't believe it worked themselves. The three men that was in the kitchen laid on the floor without any resistance.

Honcho took off upstairs, while Hondo and Sauce zip tied the three guys.

"These mafuckas ain't no cops."

Hondo kicked the guy in his mouth. "Good guess dick head. Now shut the fuck up."

Honcho came back down stairs with two crying females that he had zip tied. "Sit. Don't move."

They rolled the guys over. None of them was London.

"Yo, this the nigga from the Park Heights," Hondo said.

Sauce got a good look at the guy and smiled. It was the same guy that he shot a few months ago up Park Heights.

"Where the fuck is London?" Honcho asked. No one said a word.

Sauce put his gun to Sass's forehead. He was determined to kill him this time. "Anybody wanna answer my man?"

They remained silent. **Bow!** The tears started flowing then. Sauce put the gun to the next guy's head, after obliterating Sass's head.

"Let's try this again."

"He left with Maniac an hour ago," one of the women said.
"Where were they going?"
"I heard him talking on the phone to someone about where some twins might be hiding out," another female said.
"And he didn't tell ya'll where he was going?" Honcho asked.
"He probably told Sass," the other girl said.
Hondo pointed the gun at the women. "Ya'll ain't see shit right?" They nodded.
Honcho held up their IDs. Hondo shot the remaining two guys in the head.
"What about now? You still ain't see shit right?"
They nodded, crying. They left the women alive and left.

Hondo's phone rung when they pulled off. He saw Ivyana's number.
"Yeah baby."
"AT is dead!" she screamed, and began crying uncontrollably.

Chapter 21

Honcho's house...
(30 minutes ago)

Tamera passed everyone a glass with the expensive Rose' inside to calm their nerves. Ivyana needed the drink. She was worried about Hondo. Tammy was anxious. She wanted to be in the streets with her sons. Sitting still while her sons put in work wasn't her style. Iyana sat quietly, sipping her drink, anxiously wanting to get back to DC to handle her business. Her sister was her priority though.

The doorbell rung.

"I got it," Tammy said. "It's Delvon. I told him to get me some reefer."

"You smoke too Momma TT?"

"Sure do," she said and left the kitchen.

"Aye sis, you know we got business to handle back home."

"I know Iya. I called Eddie Rob and Nate and told them we'd be a few more days. They was cool with it."

"I bet they was. Them two crazy ma'fuckas love running loose in South East," Iyana said.

Five minutes later, Tammy still hadn't resurfaced.

"What she smoking it outside AT?"

"She can smoke in here. She know that."

Iyana got up and went to find Tammy. She hadn't smoked since she been back in Baltimore.

The front door was wide open, she went to step out the door when she felt a presence behind her.

"Do exactly as I say. Do anything else and I'm puttin' two in your wig."

Any other time she would've shot back a smart comment about her hair being real, but she knew it wasn't the time.

"How many people are in there?"

"Two more."

"Who?"

"Two females."

"Where's Hondo and Honcho?"

"They not here."

"You lying to me bitch?"

"No."

"Let's go," he said, pushing the gun on her head. "Take me to them."

When Tamera looked up, she got the shock of her life. "London, what the fuck are you doing here?!" she loudly asked.

"You know why the fuck I'm here AT. Don't play no fuckin' games with me," he said, with his hand gripping Iyana's shirt and his right hand held the gun that was pressed to the back of her head.

"We can talk about—"

"Talk!?" he barked. "Don't move no more AT. I know you… better than you know ya self. You move again I'mma kill you."

"You'd really kill the woman you love? The woman who miscarried your child twice? Me? AT?"

He looked her in the eyes and said, "You motherfuckin' right. In a heart beat."

"Where's my fuckin' sister?"

Ivyana came out the dinning room and froze.

"Oh, another twin. Get the fuck over here and sit down. Try something and umma put a bullet in ya sister's head."

"London, where is my sister?"

"She's in my truck out cold. She tried to scream when she seen me at the door, so I had to knock her ass out."

"London, you put your hands on my sister? You do know better than that don't you?"

"Fuck you AT, bitch! This ain't back in the day. I run this fuckin' city. You motherfuckas killed my son," he spit. "The only reason you ain't dead now 'cause I want your pussy-ass nephews. Now where are they?"

"You know better than that too London," she said, smiling. "You claim you know me better than I know myself. Then you should know I'd die before I tell your bitch-ass anything about my nephews."

"Your words, not mine," London said, pointing the gun at her.

"Wait!" Ivyana screamed. "You're really going to kill her? She's your family."

"I thought that too, until she killed my son."

"She didn't kill your son, but didn't you also kill her sister's baby father?"

"I-I-I don't know what you think you know little girl. Who the fuck are you anyway?"

"Naw nigga. Don't switch the subject now," Tamera said. "You jealous, weak, piece of shit. You killed Clyde 'cause you wanted to be him. You wanted to be the man. Where was family then? Huh pussy? Yousa bitch. I should've fucked you ... bitch. Put'cha legs up on my shoulders and fucked you in the buck. Bitch ass nigga. You'll never be the man Clyde was. Even now, Clyde's more man than you six feet deep than you ever was."

Bock!

Tamera's body crumpled to the floor. A single, well placed, bullet hole rested in the center of her forehead.

Ivyana started screaming and crying. Ivyana just looked on at her sister, hoping he didn't kill her.

London pointed the gun at Ivyana.

"Please don't kill my sister."

"Today is ya'll lucky day. I'm feeling a little generous. You live for now." he said. "Tell the twins I'm tired of this hide-and-go-seek shit. Their lives for their mother and your sister's life. I think that's fair enough."

"Nooo."

"No?" London questioned.

"It's okay sis. Let the twins know.I'm good. They'll go wherever for their mother, just like you'll go anywhere for me."

Ivyana nodded her head. She mouthed the words I love you and Iyana did it back.

"Tell the twins meet me at their father's grave site in two hours. No guns. No police. No bullshit. Or they're dead. You understand?"

She nodded her head. London left the house with Iyana at gun point. Ivyana grabbed her phone and ran over to Tamera.

Chapter 22

The twins didn't shed one tear as she told them the whole story. They couldn't. They were too consumed by anger, hatred, and revenge. It coursed through their bodies like electricity.

Once she was done, she stood up and said, "Let's go. It's been almost an hour."

"You not going."

"I am going Honcho. And you can't stop me. My sister is out there too."

Hondo sighed. "Aiight, come on."

"I'm going."

"Sauce, stay here with AT, And Delvon is out in his car with his neck slit."

"What if ya'll don't come back?" he asked and they knew it was a legitimate question.

"Well, you know where everything at," Hondo said. "Call K and tell'em come out here with you."

"Aiight."

The three of them went to Honcho's Range Rover Velar, but not before making their way to AT's arsenal of weapons, accessories, and ammunition.

They were all fully prepared to die at the cemetery. For their love ones it wasn't even a question, but London had to go as well. It was imperative that he lost his life at the cemetery, because their chances of ever getting him again was slim to none with the feds on his back, they understood and was ready.

They parked outside of the cemetery and got out, unaware of the car that had been following them since they pulled out of Honcho's driveway."

"What's the plan here?" Honcho asked.

"It's a guy that works here, that your mother knows. Think he can help?"

"George? Naw. Then we'd have to kill'em. We got this," Hondo said. "Let's go."

They pulled their guns out and walked in the cemetery.

"Stop. That's close enough. What did I say about the guns? You niggas was always hard headed."

"Aye London, you gotta know that you ain't leaving here alive."

"I came here knowing full well I wasn't leaving alive. So where that leaves us?"

"Shit, we might as well start shooting," Honcho said.

"That's right son. Air his ass out."

"Ya'll just like this crazy bitch."

Hondo and Honcho raised their guns.

"Wait, I'm not tryna die," Iyana said.

London raised his free hand. He had a look of confusion on his face. He raised his free hand again. "What the fuck?" he mumbled. He raised his hand once more.

"He's not coming London." Everyone faced the voice that came out of the shadows, holding a Glock .40 and a AK-47. "He's unconscious and cuffed back there."

"Fuck is you doing here bitch?"

"That bitch stay poppin' up somewhere," Tammy said.

"I'm gonna need everyone to put their guns down, now."

"I ain't doing shit," London barked.

"Detective Altman?" Honcho said, when she came into view.

Ivyana recognized her immediately as the police woman that Tammy beat up.

"The feds are looking for you as we speak. You are going to prison. And they just charged you with Clyde's murder."

He looked at the twins.

"Don't look at us bitch, we ain't snitch."

"Your baby mother told," Tammy said. "Latoya." London sighed and then laughed. "Sorry Sandra, I ain't going to jail."

"Sandra?" Ivyana and Iyana said at the same time. All eyes went on them now.

"Ivyana and Iyana Richardson." Detective Sandra Altman said.

"You know them Sandra?"

"Yes London, I do. They are my daughters. Our daughters London."

"Fuck outta here," he laughed. "Bullshit, you miscarried just like AT did."

"Yes. I lied and told you I miscarried, because you wanted to be a drug dealer and I wanted a career in law enforcement. Besides, you were cheating with Latoya and I was with Clyde."

"And you gave us to a fuckin' junkie and went on living ya life."

"I paid for everything ya'll ever did in your lives. I gave May Richardson what ever ya'll wanted."

"Bitch, fuck your money!" Iyana said.

"You can feel how you want, but you're gonna respect me," Sandra said.

Ivyana raised her gun. **Bock! Bock! Bock!** Iyana used the shots as a distraction. She kicked London's hand and dove on Tammy, moving her out the way.

Boom! Boom! Boom! Bock! Bock! Bock!

The twins stood over top of London and emptied their clips in him.

"Get these fuckin' things off me somebody! This shit hurt! My arm already broke!"

Ivyana ran over to her sister and Tammy and helped them.

"I gotta go back to the hospital, I can't feel my arm."

"Momma."

"What?"

"London killed AT," Hondo said.

Tammy lost her breath for a second, clutching her chest. She relaxed herself after a few seconds, walked over to London's still corpse and lost her composure.

Hondo's pain was real. It finally hit him that his aunt was gone. He walked off crying.

"You good sis?"

"Go get your man, Ivy."

"Ivyana ran behind him. Iyana walked over to her mother and looked at her. She didn't see any blood at all. She stooped down and tapped her mother's chest.

"Aye Honcho, she had a vest on. She just knocked out."

Honcho walked over with his mother in his arm. "What'cha gon' do? It's up to you. Just keep in mind, ya sister did put three in her chest."

"Gimmie your gun," she said.

"Look bro," Hondo said. He was holding Maniac up. "I found him by that tree over there," he said, with tears still in his eyes.

"She still alive Ivy."

"Gimmie the gun," Tammy said. She got the gun from Iyana.

Boom! Boom! Boom! She made sure Maniac was dead with three shots to his head. Tammy was angry and showed it when she started kicking London's body again.

"Come on Momma," Honcho said.

"So what's up? What'chall gon' do with ya'll mother?"

"This bitch ain't our mother," Ivyana said.

"Gimmie the gun Ms.Tammy."

Tammy gave the gun to Iyana. They all watched her. They figured out what she was doing seconds later.

Bock! Bock! Bock! Boom! Boom! Boom!

***

Ivyana went to the hospital with Tammy, while Hondo, Honcho, and Iyana went back to Hondo's to clean up. They were filthy after digging those graves in the woods across from the cemetery.

They didn't see K when they walked in, but Sauce was still there. They dapped him up and told him they'd get up with him soon. He understood.

They put everything they had on in one trash bag and Hondo left with it, leaving Iyana and Honcho alone.

He gave her some of his clothes and went to walk out when she called out, "Don't leave me alone."

Honcho sat on his bed. "I had my AT my whole life. She taught me and bro everything we know. How to hustle, how to save our money, how to shoot, how to talk to women."

He didn't know he was crying until Iyana put her arms around him.

"I'm not gonna sit her and say shit gonna be okay, 'cause it won't be… for a while. What I will say is, I'll be here for you every step of the way," she said. "When I was a little girl, I use to envision me welcoming my biological parents with open arms, but then I grew up. I don't feel no type of way about Sandra, she been dead to me anyway. London, although he didn't know about us, he was a pieces of shit and I hate him for not being there and also for causing ya'll so much pain."

He kissed her head. She raised her face to meet his. Both of their tears stained faces full of pain and grief, locked into the most passionate kiss either one of them had ever experienced.

Chapter 23

After they were clean and the house was clean, they called the police. The polices showed up and did what they were paid to do. Once word got out, amongst the police, that one of the twins from Odonnell Heights was shot and killed, the top brass wanted answers, given the story that Detective James Woody told his boss. They figured London Grundy Senior was responsible for the two murders and wanted him found. They had a BOLO (Be On The Look Out) and a APB (All Points Bulletin) out on him. The feds also cast a net over Baltimore City, looking for him. London's face aired every hour on the hour for seven days straight. By then, the whole city knew who London Grundy Senior was.

***

After AT's big funeral, they tried to go back to their normal, but it was hard. Tamera AT Huntley was a main artery inside their family. They were still sulking over the face that she was no longer with them.

All the tragedy that surrounded them did one good thing; brung Honcho and Iyana together. They helped one another cope with their issues. A match made from death, that was bonded by blood, is what they were.

***

An Apartment In Bel Air Maryland...

Closed in, away from civilization, after the hurt and pain she suffered by the hands of her family was too much to bare at times. She often found herself crying, with her 38 Revolver in her mouth, unable to pull the trigger.

She didn't understand how she lost everything so quick. She wished everyday that her daughter's three shots would've made their way to her head and not her vest. Then there was the; piece of paper that served as a reminder that there was nothing she could do about it. She was left to deal with the hand she dealt herself. No job, no family, no career; no life.

She cried and put the gun in her mouth. Her trigger finger twitched.

She threw the gun across the room. "Shit!"

Sandra laid back on her bed and closed her eyes. She was back in her car on the night her life changed.

She woke up grabbing her chest where the three bullets hit her chest. She wasn't surprised that her daughter tried to kill her. The twins came out her womb kicking, screaming, and angry. Like they knew she was going to give them up.

Why was I still breathing and in my car, she thought. Her answer laid on the passenger seat of her 2017 Audi. She picked the paper up and read it.

Yeah, you should be dead, but we rather you live a lonely life with your decisions. You will leave us alone. You won't watch us, contact us, investigate us, or even look at us if you run across us. If you do, your police friends will find the guns you used to kill London and his homeboy. If that's not enough to hold you, with your prints on the guns, maybe the bodies with the guns will. Enjoy life BITCH!

After reading the note, that's when she realized she had made the worst mistake of her life by giving up her daughters.

Seeing the pain and confusion on her daughters' faces that night felt like bullets themselves. She knew she messed up and wanted more than anything to have her daughters back in her life. Ex-detective Sandra Altman, mother of Ivyana and Iyana and baby mother of the late London Grundy Senior, knew that there was no chance in hell that her daughters would accept her back in their life, but she could make sure they were safe from a distance.

She jumped out the bed, went to her dresser, and pulled out a stack of eight by eleven photos from her personal investigation on London Senior. She chose fifteen of the thirty-five photos, put them in a manila envelope, filled it out and left out to go to the post office.

Epilogue

(June 2018)
Odonnell Heights Projects...

The projects was live. Everyone came out to celebrate the lives of everyone they lost over the past year and also celebrate the life of Shyasia and Eeyore's new born son; Russell McGowan Junior aka baby Eeyore.

They had Jamaican J's uncle, General on the grill whipping up classic curry dishes. Hondo had purchased a bulk of t-shirts that he had made with Crystal, Eeyore, Jamaican J, and AT's face on it, with Odonnell Heights Projects exposed on the back of it. Every person in the projects, at the party, wore one.

K was walking around with Baby Eeyore, showing him off. The baby was collecting a bunch of money from everyone at the party.

Hondo and Ivyana was chatting with Gia, who was back in Baltimore with her sons. They were trying to set up a date for a threesome.

Sauce and Ko Ko was boo'd up, dancing in front of the DJ's set up, having a ball.

Honcho and Iyana was talking to Tammy, as she nursed a glass of Patron.

Kim, Kia, Bird, Shyasia, and Nay-Nay sat around gossiping, doing what they do best.

Everyone was enjoying themselves. The sun went down and that's when the fun really began. The kids was put to bed and everyone else met up at Crystal's, grabbed their balloons and candles and walked over to the Holabird Elementary School to have a private candle light vigil.

Kia, Bird, Nay-Nay, Ko Ko, Kim, Hondo, General, Honcho, Sauce, Ivyana, Shyasia, Tammy, Iyana, and K was present in the school's parking lot.

"Yo, we endured a lot over the past year," Sauce began, "and we lost a few of our family, but we pushed through and gained some additions to our family," he said, looking at the twin girls.

"Yeah, we all been knowing one another since we were born—"

"I'm sorry ya'll, I just hate bitch-ass niggas," Tammy slurred. She had been drinking all day, so everyone understood.

"Yeah, we all hate bitch-ass niggas Momma."

"Aiight then Honcho. Fuck is we waitin' for, let's get to it," she said, pulling out a big, black, scary looking MP5 out of her Herme's bag.

Everyone gasp.

"Hold up Momma," Hondo said. "As I was saying, we've all been knowing each other since we were kids."

Only a few people was paying attention to Hondo, the rest was focused on Tammy and her gun. Ivyana, Honcho and Iyana eased guns out too, that was now visible to the group. Each of their guns had laser beams on them too.

"What's going on Hondo?" Nay-Nay asked.

"Ain't it obvious?"

"Hell naw," she said.

"I thought about this shit in my head, over and over and over again," he said, scratching his head. "Jamaican J. My aunt. How the fuck are they dead?"

"Yeah, I couldn't figure that out myself," Honcho said. "Jamaican J wasn't stupid. And I couldn't figure out how the fuck London knew where my house was at, when nobody knew where my shit was at, except for AT, my mother, Hondo, Ivyana, and Sauce. Not even K knew where it was when I called him to ask him why didn't he come out to my house with Sauce, the night of AT's murder."

"So what you sayin' bro?" Sauce asked. "That leaves me and Ivyana."

Hondo pulled a gun out and pointed it at Sauce, with the red beam resting on his forehead. Then four more beams was trained on him.

"Ko Ko, these niggas pussy-whipped."

"Are they," she questioned.

"Aye Ko Ko," Hondo said, "show everyone what you saw."

Ko Ko went in her bag and pulled out a manila envelope and passed it around.

"What'chall looking at, is the pussy-ass nigga interacting with the enemy. If you look at two of the dates, you'll notice they were on the days Jamaican J and AT got killed."

"Bomba clad batty boy!" General yelled.

"Why Sauce?" Nay-Nay asked.

"You let niggas kill a woman that was like a mother to you." K said. "AT gave all of us nothing but opportunities and love."

"He wasn't suppose to kill AT. He was only suppose to kill the twin bitches."

"Why Sauce?"

"You know why. She had me kidnapped."

"My sister dead because ya pussy-ass couldn't take a few punches and slaps?" Tammy yelled.

"I'm not forcing ya'll to stay. Ya'll can let ya'll balloons go and leave, while we handle this shit."

No one moved.

"You stay, you shoot," Tammy said.

"Ya'll joking right?" Sauce asked.

Bock! Tammy shot first. **Bock! Bock! Bock! Bock!** Then Hondo, Honcho, Ivyana, and Iyana. Everyone else in the circle grabbed their gun and let off a shot. General let off two shots in Sauce.

"Odonnell Heights is family. We ain't never letting no one touch our family," Tammy said. "And if you family and allow anyone to violate family, then you'll end up like this bitch-ass nigga." **Bock! Bock! Bock! Bock**! "Pussy!"

They all let their balloons go and walked back to the projects.

OTHER BOOKS BY KAYO

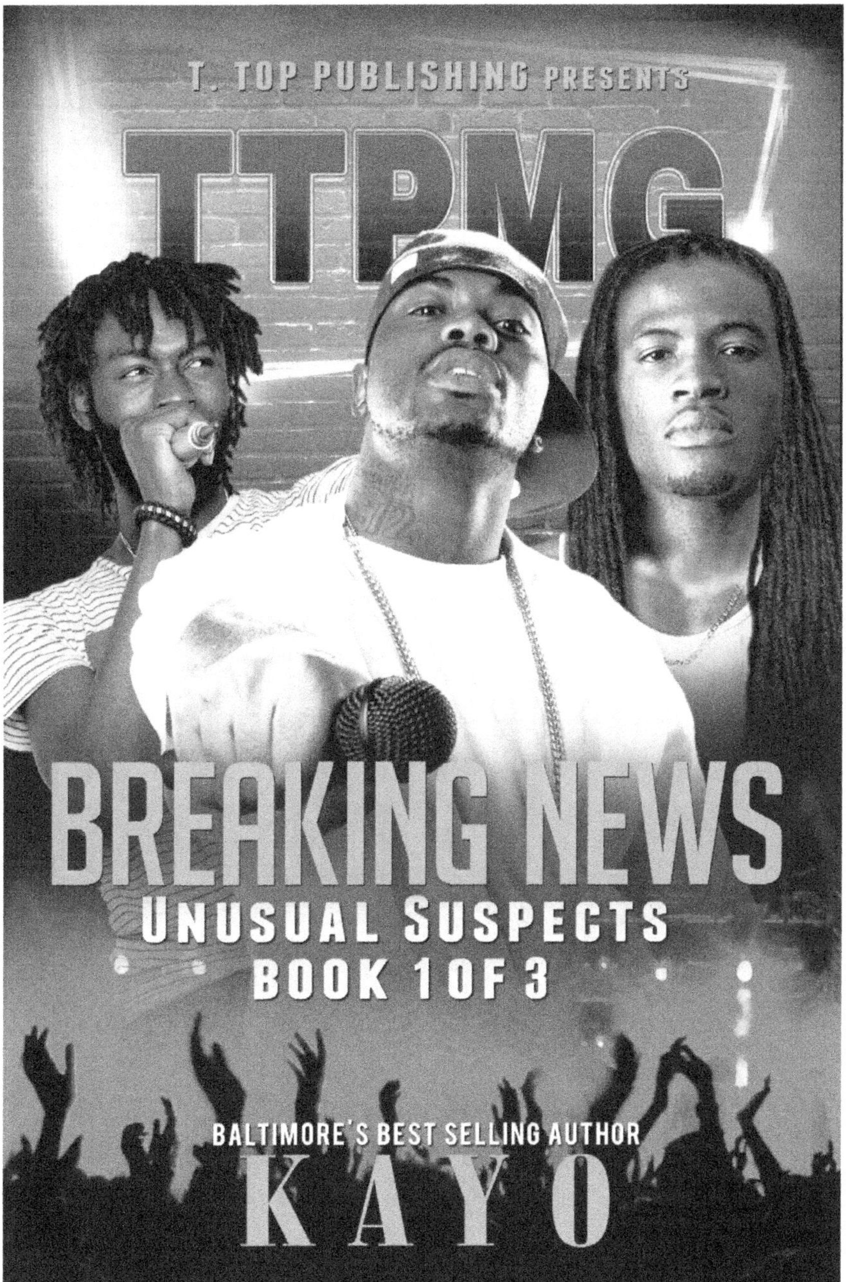
T. TOP PUBLISHING PRESENTS
TTPMG
BREAKING NEWS
UNUSUAL SUSPECTS
BOOK 1 OF 3
BALTIMORE'S BEST SELLING AUTHOR
KAYO

T. TOP PUBLISHING PRESENTS
2
BREAKING NEWS
BOOK 2 OF 3
BALTIMORE'S BEST SELLING AUTHOR
KAYO

T. TOP PUBLISHING PRESENTS
FRIENEMIES
Who Kan You Trust
BOOK 1 OF 10
BALTIMORE'S BEST SELLING AUTHOR
KAYO

T. TOP PUBLISHING PRESENTS
FRIENEMIES 2
Shhh Stop Snitchin'
BOOK 2 OF 10
BALTIMORE'S BEST SELLING AUTHOR
KAYO

T. TOP PUBLISHING PRESENTS
887
667
FRIENEMIES
3
Still Kan't Trust Nobody
BOOK 3 OF 10
BALTIMORE'S BEST SELLING AUTHOR
KAYO

T. TOP PUBLISHING PRESENTS
4 HUNNID
FRIENEMIES 4
4 Ever Tree Top
BOOK 4 OF 10
BALTIMORE'S BEST SELLING AUTHOR
KAYO

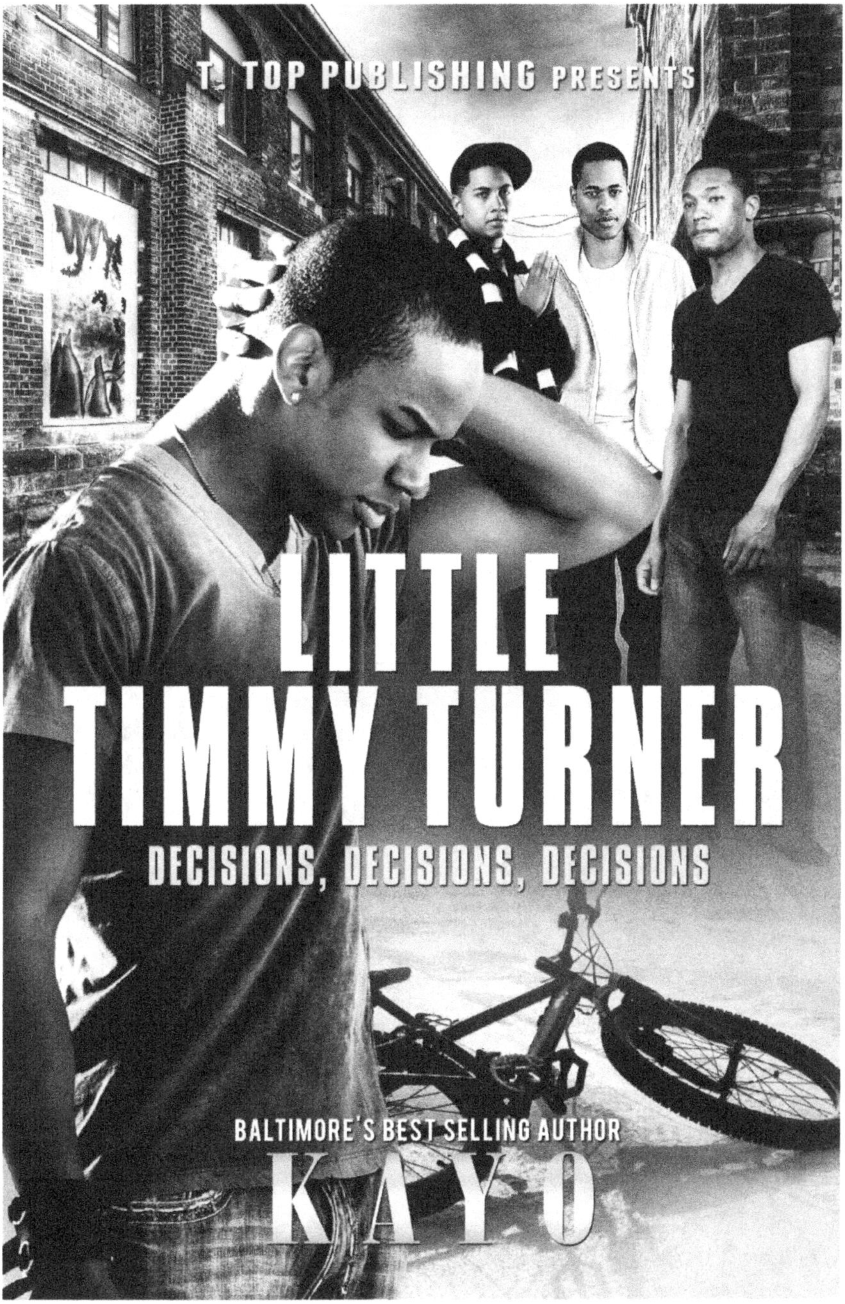
T. TOP PUBLISHING PRESENTS
LITTLE
TIMMY TURNER
DECISIONS, DECISIONS, DECISIONS
BALTIMORE'S BEST SELLING AUTHOR
KAYO

T. TOP PUBLISHING PRESENTS
She's My ROCK
MEECHIE & KYRA
BALTIMORE'S BEST SELLING AUTHOR
KAYO

T. TOP PUBLISHING PRESENTS

Hoodrat
VS
CHICKENHEAD
"The Difference"

BALTIMORE'S BEST SELLING AUTHOR

KAYO

COMING

SOON

T. TOP PUBLISHING PRESENTS

BREAKING NEWS
BOOK 3 OF 3

BALTIMORE'S BEST SELLING AUTHOR
KAYO

T. TOP PUBLISHING PRESENTS
POL
City Of
GODZ
KILLER SEASON
BALTIMORE'S BEST SELLING AUTHOR
KAYO

T. TOP PUBLISHING PRESENTS

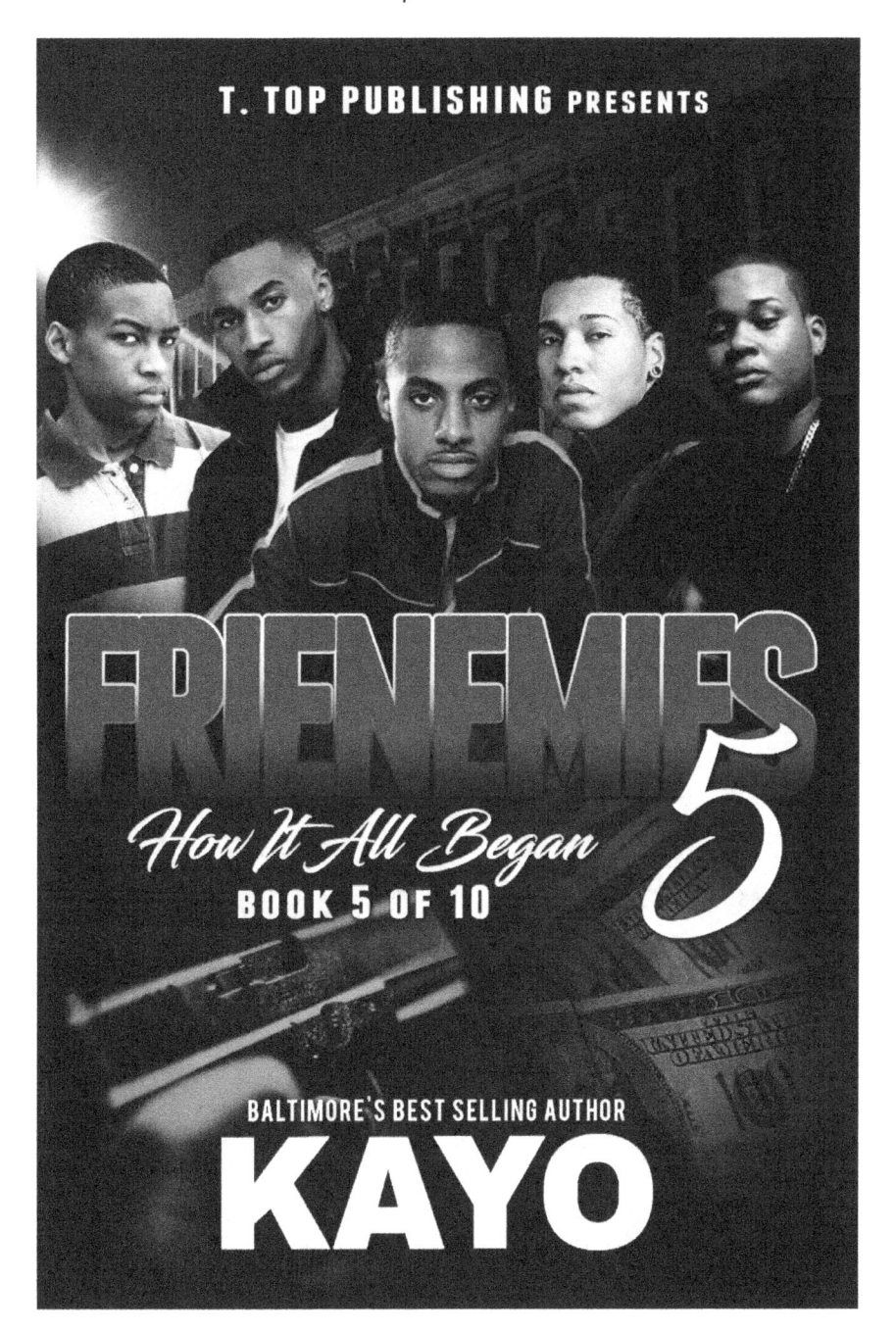

FRIENEMIES 5
How It All Began
BOOK 5 OF 10

BALTIMORE'S BEST SELLING AUTHOR

KAYO

T. TOP PUBLISHING PRESENTS

FRIENEMIES 6

Goon Affiliated

BOOK 6 OF 10

BALTIMORE'S BEST SELLING AUTHOR

KAYO

T. TOP PUBLISHING PRESENTS
FOURS
N.A.S.
Niggas Ain't Shit
'A STORY FOR ALL'
BALTIMORE'S BEST SELLING AUTHOR
KAYO

T. TOP PUBLISHING PRESENTS
THA TWINZ
REALLY WITH THE SHITS
BOOK 1 OF 2
BALTIMORE
POLICE
BALTIMORE'S BEST SELLING AUTHOR
KAYO